CHARM OFFENSIVE

A WITCHES THREE COZY MYSTERY

CATE MARTIN

CHAPTER 1

I was in the wrong place at the wrong time.

And as a witch who can travel ninety-one years into the past, when I say the wrong time, I mean the wrong century.

I had fallen asleep at Edward's apartment.

Again.

I had been floating in that place between awake and asleep for a while now, but nothing had felt seriously out of place. Sure, the smell was wrong. Back home smelled of lemony furniture polish and the distant aroma of Mr. Trevor's favorite dark roast coffee. Edward's apartment smelled of motor oil from the garage downstairs with an undertone of horse that had never left since the garage had been a carriage house. But I was used to that smell now. In that not-quite-awake space, it didn't feel wrong enough to cause any alarm.

Neither did the sound of early morning traffic on Summit Avenue, and the talking and laughing children walking in groups to school. Kids are kids no matter what the era, and from a block away the hum of so many cars was no more than white noise.

But then a single car turned down Maiden Lane and passed by Edward's window, and just like that, I was wide awake.

The puttering of that engine, the mechanical lurch of its parking brake when it stopped half a block down, had been nothing like even the most out-of-tune modern car engine.

I opened my eyes to find myself on Edward's couch. I had slipped my shoes off to curl my feet up on the cushion. Someone had taken the blanket from Edward's bed and thrown it over me.

Someone who really should have just woken me up and sent me home. How late had we been up, going over the same paltry information and multitudes of worrisome possibilities?

For that matter, how late was it now?

I tried to look back through the window behind me, but the moment I stirred, every muscle in my body shrieked in protest. It was not a comfortable couch, and my legs, in particular, were very angry about their lack of blood flow. My body wanted to contract like a pill bug not happy at being poked, but even that little bit of movement I had managed had been enough to dislodge the blanket from around my shoulders and the chill of the morning air was as sudden as a plunge into a lake fed by a cold spring.

But it cleared my mind of the last vestiges of sleep better than a double espresso.

Moving more slowly and deliberately this time, I twisted to look out through the window behind me. The window didn't open, and being over the garage door and not the staircase, there was no way to reach it to clean the accumulation of sooty streaks that darkened the panes. But I had woken up here often enough to be able to tell it was only just past dawn, the sun not yet high enough in the sky to clear the rooftops of the tall houses on Summit Avenue and reach the deeper shadows of Maiden Lane.

Early enough that Mr. Trevor wouldn't miss me unless he checked my room. And he would need some dire emergency to go looking for me there. He respected all of our privacy too much for that. None of us had ever seen him on the third floor at all after that first day at Miss Zenobia Weekes' Charm School for Exceptional Young Ladies when he had given us the house tour.

Still, it had gotten past the point where I could promise myself not to make falling asleep at Edward's place a habit. It *was* a habit.

But it was a habit I would have to break before Sophie and Brianna came back home.

I straightened my legs out, bracing for the pins and needles as the blood flow was restored to my icy feet, and became aware of two things at once.

The first was a weight on my shoulder.

The second was the taste in my mouth. In my effort not to make sleeping over a habit, I refused to bring a toothbrush with me when I went to 1928. I regretted it every time. My teeth were decidedly fuzzy, and the taste of the late-night coffee was lingering bitterly on my tongue.

Otto's coffee preferences were not as delightful as Mr. Trevor's. To him, it was a highly caffeinated fuel to be consumed, not something to linger over, savoring the complex aroma of the finest beans roasted to perfection.

A garbled sort of noise came from the weight on my shoulder, and I shifted to look down at the top of Edward's head just before he sat up with a start.

"Again?" he said, blinking as he looked around the apartment as if horrified to find himself there.

"Again," I said. "At least you grabbed a blanket this time."

He looked down at the blanket tucked around us in confusion. "I didn't. I'm pretty sure I fell asleep before you did."

"Did you?" I asked, trying to remember the night before. I sat forward and looked at the bits of paper scattered over the table.

"I did," he said, more confidently this time. "You did that spell thing on Otto's map, and then the two of you were discussing whether the fact that you didn't find any hidey holes meant there weren't any hidey holes, and after that, it's all a blur."

It took me a moment to place when that had happened. It had been relatively early in the evening, soon after we'd eaten the takeout Indian food I had brought with me from 2019. How long had it been just Otto and me talking?

What I was thinking must have been showing on my face, because Edward gave me a sly smile. "You didn't even notice I was asleep, did you?" he teased.

I tried to stammer a response, but I had nothing.

"For hours and hours," he said.

"It wasn't that long," I said, but I was afraid it really had been hours. "You didn't miss much. You saw the spell didn't really help, and we just hashed over what we've hashed over a thousand times before."

"Sure," he said. "Coffee?"

"Please," I said, mostly because making coffee would mean stoking up the stove enough to push back some of the chill. Edward slipped out from under the blanket and crossed the room to the corner that was as close as he came to having a kitchen. "But I can't stay long. I have to get back before the morning call."

While Edward filled the kettle and set it to boil, then spooned coffee into his coffeepot, I put on my shoes then gathered up the blanket. I was just spreading it back out over the bed when there was a sharp knock on the apartment door. I knew by the sound it had to be Otto, and indeed he didn't wait for an answer before letting himself inside.

"Ah, still here," he said, smirking at me.

"You could've woken me," I said as I smoothed the blanket flat.

"You weren't asleep when I left," he said. "Well, not quite. You were a bit mumbly, but you said you were fine where you were. Who am I to argue with a witch?"

"You're not afraid to argue with me," I said.

"Aren't I?" he asked.

"What time did you leave?" Edward asked.

"Three in the morning?" Otto said with a frown that said he wasn't exactly sure. "I had some business to tend to."

I looked at my watch. It was just past seven. "You slept fast."

Otto scoffed. "I haven't slept yet," he said. "Although it is almost my bedtime."

"So why are you here?" Edward asked as he poured steaming water over the coffee grounds.

"I brought you some breakfast," he said, setting a paper bag on the table on top of the map we had been poring over the night before. "Hard sausage and bread. That one is getting too thin."

I looked over at Edward, who was indeed looking thinner. I hadn't noticed until Otto pointed it out. He was paler, too. And he had conked out awfully early the night before.

"He is," I said. "Edward, are you feeling all right?"

"I'm fine," Edward said. Then flushed dark pink as Otto and I kept looking him over. "A bit tired, maybe, but fine."

"He never was a night owl," Otto told me.

"I can't have an eight a.m. bedtime with a day job," Edward said, crossing his arms defensively.

"You'd make more working for me," Otto said. "And I wouldn't care when you work. It's not like you need to keep an honest job now that..." He broke off in a rare display of tact, but we all knew what he had been about to say.

Now that Edward no longer needed to impress some upper-class potential father-in-law.

"I happen to like honest work," Edward said, adding a third mug to the other two on the table before pouring out the coffee. I could tell by the way he wasn't quite looking at either of us that he was still feeling defensive, and I shot Otto a pleading look.

"It suits you," he said. Grudgingly, but Edward's smile in return was genuine.

The fresh but bitter coffee did nothing for the unbrushed taste in my mouth, but at least the bread was good, eggy and dense and still warm from the oven.

"Did you have news?" I asked Otto. I doubted he had come out of his way just to bring us breakfast, although if he had come by just to be sure I woke up on time, he would never say so.

"We talked about casting a wider net," Otto said, holding his half-eaten roll in his teeth as he pulled another map out of the inside of his jacket and spread it out on the table.

"Outside of the Twin Cities," I said. Memory of the conversation was starting to emerge from a mishmash of dream images.

"Exactly," he said around the roll still in his teeth and pulled out another map. When he had laid it next to the first, I saw that one was of the entire state of Minnesota, the other of Wisconsin. Otto took the roll out of his mouth and started to point to various locations on the maps. "I have boys from different places, and they have connections back home. I haven't talked to everyone yet, but so far I've got Rochester, Chippewa Falls, Mankato, and Duluth for sure."

"Big net," Edward said.

"Maybe too big," I said.

"Agreed," Otto said to me. "But as I said, I've only talked to the few I've seen since I left here. I should have a good lock on the towns around here once I've checked in with my whole crew. If those witches are lying low anywhere within a hundred miles of here, someone will see something."

"I don't know," I said. "You saw their glamour magic for yourself. If they don't want to be seen, they won't be. Especially not by non-witches."

"We agreed to give this a try," Otto reminded me. I almost remembered agreeing to that.

Then I did remember. And I remembered the argument just before it. I remembered my own plan that he had argued me out of.

"No," Otto said. Apparently, my eyes had lit up with the realization.

"What's a no?" Edward asked.

"We agreed it was a no," Otto said, ignoring Edward, his eyes boring into mine.

"'Agreed' might be too strong a word," I said.

"We agreed," Otto said. "I said no way unless Sophie and Brianna were here to give you back up. Then you said they don't even know you've been coming here, and you didn't want them to know."

"What?" Edward asked, alarmed.

"I don't need backup," I said. It was only when Otto took half a step back that I realized I had my wand in my hand. I put it away hastily.

"The others don't know you've been coming here?" Edward asked.

"I told you they were out of town," I said. "Brianna is still in Boston, and Sophie is in New Orleans." I glanced at my watch. "And I've got to get back or I'm going to miss our conference call."

"Amanda!" Edward objected as I snatched a sausage out of the bag and headed for the door.

"I'm really late," I said.

"We have to talk about this," he said, putting his hand on the door to hold it shut before I could even reach the handle.

"I know, and we will," I said. "Just not right now. I have to go, and you have to get to work."

"But isn't it dangerous for you to keep coming here?" he asked.

"I'm perfectly safe," I said.

Edward looked over to Otto as if for confirmation, and I got more than a little annoyed. "Look, I know how to protect myself. I've bonded with my wand now. I know you don't know what that means, but believe me, I'm not in any danger."

"From here to the charm school, probably not," Otto said to Edward.

"And you can let it go at that," I said to Otto before he started rehashing the argument from the night before, all the reasons why I couldn't just walk around the alleys of St. Paul after dark, glowing with magic like a lure fish meant to attract witches.

It wasn't a great plan, but at least it wasn't just waiting.

"Amanda," Edward said, drawing my attention back to him. He really did look like he was missing a lot of sleep. I bit my lip.

"If anything, I'm putting you in danger," I said. "They already know you. They might suspect who you are to me."

"I'll be fine," he said.

I looked over at Otto.

"I have boys watching out for him," Otto said, and Edward turned to give him a startled look. "There's two outside now, one that keeps watch on the apartment when Edward is out, and the other to follow him to work where another boy keeps watch on that building. They might not be up to fighting witches, but they are all armed and prepared to make an uproar and draw lots of attention."

"Since when?" Edward asked. We both ignored him.

"Thank you," I said to Otto.

"Hold on," Edward said. "How long have the two of you been conspiring behind my back?"

"We're just looking out for you," Otto said.

"You're not my parents," Edward all but growled.

"We're not your parents," I agreed, and gave him a decidedly not maternal kiss. Then I winked at Otto. "Keep an eye on our boy while I'm away."

"You know I will," Otto winked back. Edward was still glowering, but another kiss was enough for us to part ways on a brighter note. I took my cloak off the hook by the door and headed out into the chilly morning.

But I made sure the folds covered me completely, hood up to leave my face deep in shadows before I went down the stairs to the cobblestone road. I was not interested in drawing magical attention, not now, and especially not at Edward's front door.

It only took moments to get back to the charm school, to the backyard where the portal lurked, a mere pinpoint of magic I was sure was hidden from all but the most powerful of time witches. And I doubted there was a time witch still living as powerful as I was now.

It didn't feel like much, moving through time. I visualized it as pushing myself through molecule by molecule and reassembling myself on the other end, like using a science fiction teleporter.

I took a moment on the other end to expand my awareness, to check that no one else had tampered with the portal or any of the wards that protected the school and especially its backyard. Once in the solarium, I took off the cloak and hung it on a hook by the door.

I was always worried I'd need it in a hurry. I hadn't yet. I hadn't sensed anything magical besides myself in months. But the worry persisted.

That cloak hid me from magical sight, but it didn't do much against the wind and cold. The temperature was a touch under average in 2019, but downright frigid in 1928. I hurried to exchange my boots for warm slippers and to pull a duster-length sweater on over my 1920s clothes so I could escape the chill of the solarium for the relative warmth of the kitchen.

Mr. Trevor was accustomed to the three of us going out into the yard before dawn, and in coming back in chilled to the bone.

I felt the first stab of guilt at my subterfuge. These stabs never came in 1928, but were getting more frequent in 2019.

I wasn't exactly lying to Mr. Trevor. I didn't have to; he never asked what I was up to, especially not when it touched on anything magical.

Still, I felt a second, deeper stab when I came into the house and found him in the kitchen, pouring himself a cup of coffee.

"Good morning, Miss Amanda," he said as I emerged from the solarium. "Coffee?"

"That would be lovely," I said, perhaps laying it on a bit thick. Especially as my hands were already shaking from the caffeine-laden cup I had already had either ten minutes or ninety-one years ago. He took out another mug and set it on the counter between us before turning back to take the carafe out of the coffeemaker.

"I was just checking the portal," I said, completely unnecessarily.

"Indeed," he said, raising his brows ever so slightly.

"Yes," I said. "It's all good."

"I have no doubt," he said and turned again to put the carafe back.

"Yes," I said. The voice in the back of my head was begging me to stop talking. How could he not be suspicious when I was babbling like an idiot?

"Can I fix you anything for breakfast?" he asked.

"No. No, I'm good," I said. Then I glanced at my watch. "Actually, I have to get upstairs. Conference call."

"Please pass on my regards to Miss Brianna and Miss Sophie," he said, gathering up his coffee and the morning paper. "I do hope they'll be home soon."

"I will, and I hope so too," I said.

But about half of me was lying about that.

CHAPTER 2

With a cup of coffee in my hand, I couldn't exactly run up the stairs, but I did try to hurry my steps to the library. I hustled past Brianna's table, the sight of it bereft of its usual chaos of books, journals, pens, and abandoned cups of half-finished tea still so unsettling.

I averted my eyes from my own desk at the end of the next aisle between bookshelves. Miss Zenobia Weekes' journal waited there, still opened to the first page, all of Brianna's notes on translating and decoding the text taped helpfully to the wall over the desk. My own notebook meant to be filled with the translation only contained a few spare sentences.

I told myself that what Otto and I were working on was surely a better use of my time than sitting in the library translating an old journal in the hopes it had more secrets than we had managed to extract by interrogating the version of Miss Zenobia that lived in its pages, the one Brianna had brought to ghostly life for a brief time.

My brain knew I was right, but still, there was that tinge of guilt.

I turned down the next aisle to the desk against the far wall and sat down, setting the steaming coffee down next to the keyboard. The closest window was open a few inches, and I could hear the traffic passing by on Summit Avenue. Now that I was paying attention, it was very little like what I had heard while still half-asleep in Edward's apartment. The electric cars, in particular, made little more sound than the hiss of tires on pavement.

I really had to stop falling asleep there. Setting aside what Brianna and Sophie would say if they knew, it wasn't safe for Edward. Otto was looking out for him with all the resources he could muster, but neither of us had any illusions that those resources would be enough if that coven of witches came for Edward.

I pulled my mind back to the present and reached for the mouse, then woke the computer up to open the video conferencing program. For a moment, I only saw my own reflection in the flatscreen monitor. Walking home with my hood up had flattened some of the chaos of my hair, but not in a good way.

The program said I hadn't missed any calls. I glanced at my watch, then ran the tip of my tongue over my teeth. The flavors from the bread and sausage were lingering, but not enough to overpower last night's coffee. Worse, some of the sausage was caught in my teeth.

I scrawled "BRB" on a notecard and propped it in front of the camera, then ran, this time really ran, up to the third floor and the bathroom we all shared.

I brushed and flossed my teeth thoroughly until all that lingered on my breath was minty freshness, and nothing lurked annoyingly between my teeth. Then I brushed out my hair and twisted it back in a clip. It was out of my face, if still far from neatly arranged. Then I ran back down the stairs.

I could hear the tone of someone calling in as I jogged into the library. The computer connected, and Sophie's voice echoed through the bookshelves. "Hello?" Then, "oh," she said, apparently seeing my card. "Great."

"I'm here," I said, tossing the card aside, then pulling out the chair to sit down. There was a yowl of protest, and I turned to see our ginger cat Ziggy curled up in my seat.

"Something's up?" Sophie asked as I scooped up the still protesting Ziggy, then sat down in the chair. It was a process getting him settled on my lap. He was still annoyed at his nap being interrupted. All the cats considered the entire library their domain now that Brianna was gone. But with enough scratches around his ears, I managed to convince him to withdraw his claws from their grip on my thighs and settle down on my lap to resume his nap.

"What?" I asked, distracted by soothing the cat. "Oh, no. I just woke up late. And with weird hair."

"Your hair's fine," Sophie said, but her eyes narrowed as she looked at me more closely. What was she looking at? Did I look different? Could she tell what I had been up to? But she just sat back in her own chair, and I guessed I had passed her assessment. "Late night, then?" she asked.

"No more than usual," I said and reached for my coffee. I breathed its aroma in deeply, but set it back down without taking a sip. Its flavor would not play nice with the minty toothpaste.

"How's the weather?" she asked.

"Oh, mid-forties, I guess," I said. I came this close to saying, "warmer than in 1928," but bit it off just in time. "How about there?"

"It's supposed to get up to seventy-five or so today," she said.

"Isn't that on the cold side for there?" I asked.

"What, compared to summer, you mean?" she asked.

"I mean, it looks like you've already acclimated to the north," I said, gesturing towards the toned arms that her tank top left bare. "I bet you're surrounded by folks in sweaters."

"More hoodies than sweaters, but I get your point," she said. "Of course, Mardi Gras ended last week, but there are still a lot of tourists around. That makes for an eclectic fashion collection."

"I suppose," I said. I was about to ask if she had heard from Brianna when Brianna herself finally joined the video conversation.

"Sorry, sorry," she said, still settling into her chair. She looked like she had run to the computer. "Lost track of time."

"Something we should know about?" Sophie asked.

"No, it's fine," Brianna said.

"Does anyone have any major news?" I asked. "Any big leads or new dangers or anything?"

Brianna in Boston and Sophie in New Orleans both shook their heads.

"Nor I," I said. "So I guess this is just a status update call. Sophie, do you want to go first?"

"No news of my mother," Sophie said. "I've gone back again and again to the spot where she was taken, but no spell I've tried has told me anything more about what happened there."

"Did you try the one I sent you?" Brianna asked.

"I did," Sophie said. "I conjured something. Like a ghost of a memory. But it had too little form. I couldn't even tell what it was, let alone communicate with it. And it dissolved so quickly."

"I'm sorry," Brianna said. "I guess too much time has passed."

I shifted uncomfortably in my seat. Would I be able to tell more if I went to New Orleans and tried my own form of magic? The passage of time was no obstacle for me. Surely I could tease out the story of what had happened, or at least the rough outlines of one. I braced myself for Sophie to ask me to do just that. I didn't even know how I would respond if she did.

"It's not just time," Sophie said. "There is a lot of magic here. Now that I'm more attuned to it, it blows my mind. I thought I was sensitive before, but all I was really feeling was the most powerful of spells, the most recent, the ones more likely to directly affect me. I was missing so much."

"You think that's interfering with you finding your mother?" I asked.

"It's like trying to follow her footsteps on a beach where a marathon of runners has been since," Sophie said.

"So, are you going back to the school?" Brianna asked.

"No, not yet," Sophie said. "Unless you need me there?"

"No, I'm handling things here just fine on my own," I said. Perhaps too quickly.

"What are you working on?" Brianna asked.

"Well, I guess that marathon of runners," Sophie said. "I'm sensing patterns. Groups working magic together."

"Covens?" Brianna asked.

"I think so," Sophie said.

"What sort of magic are they casting?" I asked.

"That's what I'm trying to find out," Sophie said. "The bit I do understand about my mother's disappearance, I'm almost certain one of these covens was involved."

"One that's still active?" I asked.

"I don't know," Sophie said, shaking her head sadly. "There's so much I don't know. But I think I'm getting close on some of the big things. I really want to stay, at least for a while. If I run out of leads or things to try, I'll come right home. Sooner if you need me."

"Learn all you can," I said. "Even just learning more about how different covens work together can help us."

"I know you mean fighting Patricia and the others if we have to, but I think maybe I might learn something that connects to your mother too," Sophie said.

"How?" I asked.

"You told us your parents died in a car crash, driving in a sleet storm, right?" Sophie asked.

"That's what the Schneidermans always told me," I said.

"Oh," Brianna said, as always putting the pieces together faster than I could.

"What?" I asked. "Why does a sleet storm equal a coven of witches?"

"Maybe just one," Brianna said. "A weather witch."

"I still don't—" I started to say, but Sophie was holding up her hand, so I stopped talking.

"Your birthday is in August," Sophie said. "I know it's colder up there than it is here, but not that cold. Not in August."

"That's crazy," I said, but I felt a chill running up my spine. I pressed my hands to my temples. "I never questioned it. Never."

"I checked the historical weather reports," Sophie said. "There's no mention of it in any of the local papers. It must have been very localized."

"And layered with memory magic," Brianna said. "You grew up with that story. I bet you heard it more than once. And no one ever questioned it."

"Hence a coven," I said. "The same coven that went after your mother?"

"I have no idea," Sophie said. "But I very much want to know."

"Is there anything like that on your end?" I asked Brianna.

"It's different here," Brianna said. "My foster mothers are the only remaining members of the coven they used to lead. But like I said, most of those members weren't even really witches. It's very rare here for real witches to join into large groups."

"Why do you think that is?" I asked.

"They're older here," Brianna said. "They can look like they're forty or sixty or eighty, but once you start talking to them, you realize they were alive when the trials were happening in Salem. Some of them are far, far older than that."

"They must know all sorts of things," Sophie said.

"Things about Miss Zenobia, for starters," I said, but Brianna was shaking her head.

"They're slow to trust," she said. "It took a lot of work to get my foster moms to even introduce me to their own mentor. She told me tons of stuff—I wrote it all down so I could share it with both of you when we're together again—but nothing about Miss Zenobia. But she thought she might know someone who knows someone who knew Miss Zenobia back in the old world."

"So you've only met the one witch so far?" Sophie asked.

"I'm meeting her friend tomorrow night," Brianna said. "And if that interview goes well, she'll ask that third witch to receive me. I guess she lives pretty far underground, half removed from this world, and doesn't like visitors."

"I'd ask what that means, but I'm afraid of the answer," I said. Sophie laughed.

"Yes, well," Brianna said, flushing.

"So what part of that made you late for our call?" Sophie asked. "Or did you oversleep like Amanda?"

"No, I was here," Brianna said, and I noticed for the first time that she wasn't calling from her usual hotel room. There was no wall of bad modern art behind her.

It was books. Books that looked older even than the ones on shelves around me. And on the very top of her window on my computer screen, I could see stacks of scrolls.

"Where are you?" I asked.

"It's a library," Brianna said, but she was flushing again.

"Not a public library, I'm guessing," Sophie said.

"No, not a public library," she said. She was studiously avoiding looking into the video camera.

"Whose library is it?" I asked.

"I guess it's mine now," Brianna said. "Well, ours."

"Ours?" Sophie asked.

"Not ours, like us three. I found it with some other people. It's sort of a lost library. Or maybe hidden is the better word. There were some sizable wards protecting it."

"Is there something in this library that's going to help us figure out what happened to our mothers, or what Miss Zenobia was really up to?" Sophie asked.

"Not directly," Brianna said evasively. "But there's so much to learn here."

"It sounds like a distraction," Sophie said sternly. Brianna flushed a deep shade of crimson.

"Hey," I said. "We can trust Brianna. It sounds like the witches she's questioning are heavily invested in making her wait. At least she's making good use of her time." Brianna looked up enough to give me a tiny smile.

"Maybe," Sophie said, but both Brianna and I knew she was far from convinced. "So what about you?"

"Me?" I asked.

"You were working on translating the journal," she said. "Any luck there?"

"I'm plugging away at it," I said. "Nothing new so far. Maybe I should just skip to the end?"

"No," Brianna said. "The oldest stuff might turn out to be the most important. Don't skip around. Is it slow going?"

"Yes," I said. It was a bit of a relief, being able to say at least one thing with total honesty.

"I'll take over when I'm back," Brianna said. "But I don't know when that'll be. It depends on when that third witch will meet with me. If she will at all."

"So you might be heading back tomorrow?" I asked, carefully keeping my tone even.

"Oh, no," Brianna said. "No, I have so much to do here. We tore down the protective wards when we broke in here. I can't leave this place exposed like that. I need another week here, minimum."

"Unless Amanda gives us the call back," Sophie reminded her.

"Yes, unless she does that," Brianna agreed, but I could see how much the thought pained her.

"So I guess that's everything," I said.

"Not quite," Sophie said. "What about Nick?"

"Nick?" I asked.

Sophie's eyes were narrowing again, and now I was the one flushing pink. How had I forgotten Nick? Nick, who was working with a private investigator to find any hint of what had happened to our mothers after they had left St. Paul.

"Have you heard from him?" Sophie asked. I patted my pockets, but of course, my phone wasn't in any of them. I never took it back to 1928 to me; it was just too risky, not to mention of little use back in an age with no cell towers or Wi-Fi. It was upstairs on my nightstand, fully charged and waiting to serve me.

When was the last time I had actually looked at it, though? Days ago? Weeks?

How many missed calls had it logged, waiting for me to return? How many increasingly concerned voicemails?

"No, I haven't," I said, telling myself to calm down. If Nick were worried about me, if I weren't responding to his calls or texts, he'd just come over and knock on the door. And if he had, Mr. Trevor would have told me so.

But now I was starting to worry about why he hadn't tried to contact me. Was *he* in some sort of danger?

"Amanda?" Sophie called.

"Sorry," I said. "He hasn't contacted me, but I haven't contacted him either. I'll do that today, see what he's got even if it's nothing. I'll update you when we talk again. Earlier if he has something."

"Great!" Brianna said, and I could see she was anxious to get back to whatever she had been doing before she had sprinted to her computer. "So we're good?"

"We're good," Sophie said. The minute Brianna's window winked out, Sophie's face broke out in a fond smile. "I miss her." Then she was looking straight at me. "I miss you too, you know."

"At least you two are keeping busy, tracking down strange covens and breaking into hidden libraries," I said. "I'm just here, waiting for something to happen."

"And?" Sophie prompted.

"It never does," I said.

"I meant, and you're translating that text," Sophie said. "But I wouldn't blame you if that's going slow. It's got to be a nightmare."

"It's really more Brianna's thing," I said.

"Yes," Sophie agreed, but she sounded distracted, and when I looked up at her, she was giving me that assessing look again.

What was she seeing? Did something show on my face?

Then I realized I was dressed for 1928. I had taken off the bulky sweater when I'd gone upstairs to clean up. Now my old-fashioned skirt and sweater were on full display.

I glanced over at the little window that showed my own image as the others saw it. Only the very top of my shoulders was in frame. Surely she couldn't tell anything from that?

"Was there something else?" I asked.

"No," Sophie said, still sounding thoughtful. "I should go. But good luck with that translating. And don't forget about Nick."

"I won't," I promised, but she was already gone.

CHAPTER 3

All three of us were early risers, and we had set up the time for our conference calls around the fact that Brianna and Sophie were both in the eastern time zone, so when I glanced at my watch after Sophie hung up, I saw it was not even eight in the morning yet.

Not quite eight, and yet I felt totally ready for bed.

The coffee was room temperature by now, but I carried it with me as I headed upstairs to my bedroom. Or more specifically, to my cellphone.

The little blue light was flashing patiently, waiting for me to notice. I unplugged it from the charger and sat on the edge of the bed as I scrolled through the notifications.

So many notifications. That ready for bed feeling intensified. It would be so easy just to settle in under the covers and forget about everything, just for a few hours. Too many nights curled up on Edward's couch were taking a toll.

I had an email in my inbox from the Schneidermans. I had sent them a weekly letter every Sunday like clockwork since I had moved to St. Paul, or at least I had up until Sophie and Brianna had left on their separate missions. After three weeks with no word from me, the

Schneidermans had gotten desperate enough to use the computer in the diner office to send me an email asking me if I was okay.

I was a terrible person. Letting journal translations slide was one thing. Forgetting about Nick was another, worse thing. But forgetting the couple who had all but raised me? Unforgivable.

I changed into jeans and a sweater, then tucked my phone into my pocket before heading back to the computer in the library. I would have to answer that email first, and it would need more care and attention than I could manage typing with my thumbs.

Only when that was done and sent off to Iowa did I turn my attention to the other notifications on my phone. I had several missed calls from Nick, but no voicemails. So, no news, or news so major he didn't want to leave it in a message?

The texts were no more illuminating. Just things like "Amanda?" "You there?" "You up?"

But the last one, received just that morning while I was talking with Brianna and Sophie, said: "Can you call me?"

I was just scrolling through my contacts to get to his name when there was a knock at the front door. Phone in hand, I ran down the steps and threw open the door.

Nick was standing there with his arms full of file folders. He was trying to tug off his knit cap without disturbing something resting on top of the folders, but was not quite succeeding.

"Hey," I said. "I was just about to call you. Sorry, I've been out of touch."

"I'm sure you've been busy, what with the others away," he said. He finally got his cap off, but it had caught on one ear and came off with such force it was all he could do not to lose the folders sliding precariously in his arms. I lunged forward and caught the loose object that fell from the top of the stack before it could land on our doormat.

It was a little stuffed rabbit, one eye missing, ears rubbed nearly bare. In short, well-loved.

"Is this yours?" I asked.

"Oh, no," he said, taking the rabbit back from me and stuffing it in one of the pockets of his jacket. "It's part of why I'm here. Can I come in?"

"Of course," I said, stepping back into the foyer. He came in, then bent to untie and slip off his muddy boots. It was hard to tell in the dim foyer that received almost no sun until late afternoon, but he looked pale. And there were dark smudges under his eyes. "You look tired," I said.

"I've been doing overnight ride-alongs," he said. "That's kind of why I'm here."

"Oh," I said. "I thought it was about my mother."

"No. I'm sorry. I don't have any news there yet," he said.

"That's all right," I said. "I know these things take time. It was all so long ago."

"The P.I. has some leads. I don't know how promising they are, but it's definitely too soon to give up," he said.

"So, why are you here?" I asked, but then shook my head. "No, first let's get some food in you."

"Coffee would be great," he said.

"Coffee and food," I said. "Eggs at least."

"I would say no, but I don't think it would make any difference," he said.

"No, it won't," I said. "I'm hungry myself, so it's not really any extra trouble if that's what's holding you back. And you can explain what you have there while I cook."

"It's a deal," he said.

Nick sat down at the kitchen table and started sorting the folders into piles. As I poured the coffee, I saw most of what he had was about my mother as well as Brianna's and Sophie's. He had little hand-written notes paper-clipped to the covers here and there, but only a few sparse lines. I put a pan on the stove, then went into the refriger-ator to find the eggs.

"Here it is," he said, sounding enormously relieved. I peeked my head over the refrigerator door.

"Afraid you lost it?" I asked. His reaction seemed outsized, but perhaps that was the lack of sleep?

"You have no idea," he said with a humorless laugh.

"Not until you tell me what's going on," I said.

"It's about a lost boy," he said. "An orphan. Jackson Smith. I was hoping your magic might help me find him."

"I'll help all I can," I said. "But wouldn't I be your last resort?"

"Not in this case," he said. "He's disappeared. Like really disappeared. He doesn't exist in the computer systems. No one else who met him knows who I'm talking about when I ask about him. The only proof I have that he even exists is his case file and this stuffed rabbit. And for a minute there, I thought the case file had winked out of existence too."

"You think something magic is going on?" I asked as I mixed eggs with a dash of milk.

"It's just like before," he said. "That dead body you found next door to my grandfather's apartment. The one that disappeared from the morgue along with the wardrobe in the evidence room. The one that no one remembers but me and you three. It's exactly like that. It can't be a coincidence."

I poured the scrambled eggs into the pan, then left them to set up, taking a step closer to Nick at the kitchen table. His face was drawn, and I could easily imagine the roil of emotions turning over inside him. No wonder he wasn't eating.

"When did he disappear?" I asked.

"Sometime between early yesterday morning, like 3 or 4 a.m., and just an hour ago," he said. "He was in the back seat of his parents' car when they were hit by a drunk driver going the wrong way down a freeway ramp."

"So when you said he was an orphan, you were talking recently," I said, turning back to the eggs on the stove.

"Yes. I was in the first car to respond. He had been showered in windshield glass but wasn't really hurt. I sat with him while the first responders did what they could. But there wasn't much they could do. And the kid had no other family than his parents. No grandparents or uncles or aunts. He got dropped off with a temporary foster family. That was the last time I saw him."

"You're sure it's magic?" I pressed.

"When I got up this morning, I wanted to check on him, but the foster parents acted like they had no idea who I was talking about," Nick said. "I know it was the same people, and they struck me as good people. They weren't lying. They just didn't remember him. Like he had never been there."

"Then you checked the computer system," I guessed.

"I did," Nick said. "He was gone. I checked with the others who had been at the scene. They remembered the accident and the deceased, but not the boy who survived."

I plated up the eggs and brought them to the table, but neither of us started eating. He opened the thinnest of the folders and slid it across the table to me. On top was a photo of a child wrapped in a blanket sitting on a curb. A man in a police uniform was sitting beside him, head bent as he spoke to the boy. The tilt of his head and his uniform cap obscured his face, but I knew it was Nick.

Then I looked at the boy. He was eight or nine years old with a thick mop of dark chestnut hair. He was looking up at whoever was taking his picture. There was something so familiar about those eyes. Those haunted eyes. This was a kid who had just lost everything but was trying so hard to be brave. I could see the tracks of tears cutting through the smudges of dirt on his face, but he wasn't breaking down. He looked like a real trooper.

I don't think I took it half so well, the day my mother died. And I had been almost done with high school.

"Jackson Smith," I said, reading the name from the paperwork under the photo.

"So, what do you think?" Nick asked. "Is something magic going on?"

"It can't be the same thing that happened before," I said. "It's not possible."

"How not?" he asked.

"Well, it shouldn't be possible," I amended.

"Okay," Nick said. "Is there a way for you to be sure?"

I sighed, looking down at the plate of eggs before me. But my appetite had gone.

"Come on," I said, and led the way upstairs to the library.

I had forgotten he had never been on this floor of the house before. His eyes were huge as he looked at everything around him. The library contained far more than just books, especially since Brianna had taken over the space. A lot of the magical objects that had previously been confined to Miss Zenobia's office were now here. Most of them looked exotic and interesting but were actually quite benign.

But a few, like the glass spheres stacked in a bowl on one of the tables, were clearly far from mundane bits of bric-à-brac.

"Don't touch anything," I said.

"There's something moving in there," he said to me, his voice so soft it was a mere whisper of breath.

"There is," I said. "And we don't want to let it out."

Nick plunged his hands deep into his pockets and hurried his steps to stay close with me as I went into the farthest, darkest corner of the library.

Where we had stashed the wardrobe.

"So there's that," Nick said, recognizing the antique. "Is it still spitting out dead bodies?"

"No," I said, "and it only did that when someone stuffed one in the other end."

"The other end?" he asked.

"That's a long story," I said.

"I'd like to hear it," he said.

"Now might not be the time," I said. "I'm going to check some things here, and if I find it's been used to do harm in this time, I'll absolutely tell you the whole story."

"And if it hasn't?"

"I'll still tell you the whole story if you like, but later," I said. "I want to focus on Jackson right now."

"Me too," Nick said. "So, what do you have to check?"

"Magic stuff," I said. "Why don't you sit over there until I'm done?"

Nick looked where I was pointing and saw a winged-back reading chair tucked in the tiny corner between the library's wall and the open door to the hallway. I kind of wished I had left him downstairs to eat his eggs while I did this, but I suspected he too would have no appetite until we had some answers.

Still, I had never done magic in front of a nonmagic person before. Aside from fighting witches when Otto and Edward were there, but that had been loud, visible magic. What I was about to do was subtler.

What would it look like to Nick? Was I about to freak him out entirely? Or leave him disappointingly underwhelmed?

He was just barely okay with the fact that I was a witch. It had taken a lot of work for us to find this new equilibrium to our friendship. And even that equilibrium was still rocking back and forth, not yet steady.

And I was about to jostle it, hard.

But what choice did I have? I had never met Jackson Smith, but those eyes in that photo? I'd do anything to make things okay for that kid again.

CHAPTER 4

I sat cross-legged on the carpet in front of the Louis XV wardrobe and closed my eyes. But knowing Nick was there, watching me, was too distracting. I couldn't quiet my mind. I took a deep breath, then another. I focused on everything around me that wasn't Nick. The soft vibration from cars passing by outside the library windows. The even softer sound of three kittens purring together in their cat bed next to the cold fireplace. The smell of old books and parchment that surrounded me.

But mostly I focused on the wardrobe itself. My eyes found every chip in the wood, every scuff mark on its spindly little legs. My nose could still detect the coppery tang of blood from the gangster who had been stabbed in 1928 then traveled across time to die at my feet in the present.

Then I closed my eyes, and I was in the world of threads. The light from the wardrobe, so suffused with magic, old and new, glowed blindingly at first. But much like how eyes adjust to brightness in the real world, my awareness shifted until I was able to make out different grades in that brightness.

The old magic from the sister witches in the 1880s who had first enchanted this wardrobe still lingered, although their spell had lost all stability when the matching wardrobe had been destroyed in a fire. But the threads that lingered spoke of a spell of elegance, a longing to stay bound to each other. I knew the sisters had since grown apart, but when the spell had been woven, their love had been strong.

The witch Evanora had been the last to use the wardrobe, she and at least some of the others from Patricia's coven. Debra St. John for sure, since her specialty was magic involving memory. Not even Brianna was sure how she had done it, but somehow she had used the wardrobe as a conduit. It had been stored in the evidence room at the police station when her spells had moved through it to erase the memory of it and the gangster's dead body both from the minds of every police officer save Nick.

I checked the threads carefully, but there were no new ones. That spell had been the last to move through the wardrobe. If she had done that same memory-erasing spell across time again, she had found some other way to breach the decades between 1928 and now.

The outermost layer of spells was the brightest, both the newest and the strongest. These were the wards Brianna had cast over the wardrobe to keep the coven from using it against us. Her spellwork was precise, intricate, if not as elegant as the sisters' spells. The old spells were like the finest of calligraphy, each letter shaped by hand, quill and ink. Brianna's was more like a computer font, everything shaped exactly as it needed to be, with no variation.

Nothing had gotten through. I was pretty sure if Debra or Evanora had even tried, I would see signs of it. There would be darker, dying threads of spells that fizzled out, unable to pass the wards. But I saw nothing of the sort.

I opened my eyes, realized my head felt heavy and swimmy and put my hands out just before I face-planted on the carpet.

"Amanda?" Nick asked, as if the word had been torn from him despite his effort not to make a sound.

I took several deep breaths before answering. "I'm okay." Then a few more before my head cleared enough that I could sit back up. "I'm okay. Sometimes I get too caught up in what I'm looking at, and I forget to breathe."

"What did you see?" he asked.

I thought of all the threads I had examined, of their different characteristics and the different ways they had interacted or not with each other. I could describe it for hours and never adequately convey what I experienced in that other world.

Instead, I just said, "it's still inert."

"You mean it can't be used for magic?" he asked.

"Brianna sealed it up tight," I said. "Nothing is getting through. But even if someone tried and failed, I would see signs of that. No one did."

"Okay, but would they have to use this wardrobe to do stuff?"

"That's the real question, isn't it?" I said. Then I got up from the floor. "Come on, let's go eat and figure out what to try next."

We went back down to the kitchen, and I put our plates of now-cold eggs in the microwave. Nick sat down at the table and fidgeted with his fork.

"Look, I know I haven't been the most open to all this witch and magic stuff," he said. "And I know you've been trying to tell me just the minimum of stuff I need to know so that I don't freak out or whatever. I appreciate that."

"Okay," I said slowly. The microwave beeped, and I took out our plates. Microwaved eggs don't have the greatest texture, but at the moment, I was too hungry to care.

"I think I need the whole story now," he said. "I'm sure that what's happened to Jackson is a magic thing. I've accepted that. If I'm going to be any use to you in helping him, I have to understand things better. So I'm ready to hear all of it. If you're willing to tell me?" He glanced up at me, cheeks reddening. "I mean, maybe it's all supposed to be a secret, and you'd get in trouble for telling outsiders?"

"No, nothing like that," I said. "I'll tell you all I know. But keep in mind, I didn't know witches were real, let alone that I was one, until pretty much the day after we met."

I tried to explain everything to him, about magic and witches and wands and spells. He listened attentively, but without interrupting.

But even without a single question from him to point it out, I realized there were big gaps in my knowledge.

Like the fact that I didn't even really know where magic came from, or why some people could use it, but others apparently couldn't.

There was no way to avoid telling him how many times I'd been to 1927 and 1928, and Otto had been such a big part of so many of our investigations I couldn't leave him out either.

But I did leave out Edward and the story of the death of his fiancée. I only mentioned the last bit, where I was first aware of the coven watching me, and when I had gone back to see Coco while wearing the cloak Brianna had enchanted to hide me from their view.

As I yammered away, we polished off the eggs, then a couple of slices of buttered toast and tea, then still more tea until finally I ran out of things to say. We sat quietly for a moment, and I could practically hear his mind processing it all.

"So your magic is time travel?" he asked at last.

"Actually, Juno told me it involves seeing stories," I said. "I guess I can see what she means—that is basically what I see when I study the threads—but that doesn't feel like power to me. Manipulating those threads, that's the power. And that is more controlling time than story."

"That sounds dangerous," he said. "Manipulating time?"

"I don't do it willy-nilly," I said. "And since Brianna took Evanora's tainting spell off my wand, I've been doing all sorts of magic." To prove it, I took out my wand and tapped his teacup. The cold tea lingering at the bottom of the cup began to emit curls of steam.

"Handy," he said. "But why dismiss story magic as useless?"

"Because it is?" I said.

But Nick was shaking his head. He dug around in the pockets of his jacket until he found the stuffed rabbit and set it on the table between us. "Tell me this thing's story."

"Okay," I agreed, picking up the rabbit. I ran my fingers over its well-loved ears, over the patch on its flank where the plush was matted down, a truly aged food stain.

Then I closed my eyes and looked at it again from the world of threads.

It was like nothing I had ever seen. I had seen objects that had been severed from time; the cut ends always held a particular horror for me. I had seen objects that had been sealed off outside of time, glowing with a dark energy that couldn't touch the real world around it.

But this was neither of those things. Its threads looked perfectly normal, and they stretched out into the world around it, just like any normal object that was interconnected with everything around it.

But the rabbit's threads, long as they were, only circled back to itself. It wasn't touching anything except, by one slender thread, me and, by an even finer thread, Nick.

I opened my eyes with a gasp.

"What is it?" Nick asked, reaching out to touch my hand, still clutching the rabbit.

"That was weird," I said.

"Weird how?"

"This rabbit isn't connected to anything," I said. "Nothing except you and me."

"So it's not in the web that you see?" he asked.

"No, it isn't," I said. "But it wasn't cut away or sealed off or anything aggressive like that. It's more like... it was never a part of anything in the first place."

"But how can that be?" Nick asked.

"I don't know. This is new to me," I said.

"But this was Jackson's," Nick said. "He's too old for it now, but surely it should still be connected to him. Right? Isn't that how those threads work?"

"I would think so," I said. "I don't know for sure."

"Would it help if we went to the site of the accident? Would you see more there?" Nick asked.

"No, I don't think so," I said.

"So what can I do?" he asked.

"You already did all you could by bringing this to me," I said, giving his own hand a squeeze. "I'm not giving up. I don't know what I'll do next, but I'll think of something. I promise, we're going to find out what happened to Jackson."

"Okay," Nick said, processing again. "Okay. But when are Brianna and Sophie coming back?"

I looked down at the rabbit in my hands. That was the real question, wasn't it? Something was happening, something magical, something beyond me personally. Just the sort of situation that was supposed to prompt me to call them home.

But they were still investigating their own leads. Brianna for sure needed a few more days. Sophie might need even more time than that. And surely whatever happened to Jackson was a result of time magic, the one part of magic that was more my thing than theirs.

What if I called them back, delaying or potentially destroying their own investigations, and it was all for nothing because they couldn't even be of any help?

But what if I didn't, and then that turned out to be the wrong choice? One missing kid could just be the tip of the iceberg. If it really was the coven acting across time again, it almost certainly was part of something bigger.

"Amanda?" Nick said, and I realized I had been sitting quietly stewing for several minutes.

"I don't know when they'll be back," I said at last. "I don't want to call them back until it's absolutely necessary."

"Isn't it now?" Nick asked.

"Not yet," I said. "There's more I can do without them. If I run out of leads, I'll bring them home, but I'm not there yet."

Nick nodded glumly, then started restacking the file folders.

"You trust me, don't you?" I asked. He looked up, startled.

"Of course I do," he said. "I trust you implicitly."

"Good," I said with a smile of relief. "That goes both ways, you know."

He smiled back at me. "I didn't know. But I'm glad."

"Can I hold on to this rabbit?" I asked. "It might prove helpful."

"Absolutely," he said. Then he gestured with the stack of folders. "I'm still following up leads on this. I haven't stopped digging."

"I know you haven't," I said as we walked down the corridor towards the front door. "I'm sorry I've been hard to reach. I'm going to be checking in more now, I promise. If you have any news about Jackson or my mother, don't hesitate to call."

"I will, and you too," he said, handing me the folders so he could pull on his hiking boots and lace them back up. He straightened up, and I held out the folders, but he didn't take them right away. He just looked at me like there was something weird going on with my face.

"What?" I asked, resisting the urge to brush the corners of my mouth. Was I covered in butter or something?

"There's just something different about you," he said.

"Different how?" I asked.

"I don't know," he said. "You just look different. Hey, maybe it's because you're bonding with your wand."

"Maybe," I said, but I was certain that wasn't it.

"Have you been going back to 1928? Without the others?" he asked.

"No more than necessary," I said, nearly choking on the lie.

"Well, be careful," he said. "I know I don't understand your power, and I really don't understand what that coven can do. But promise me you'll be careful."

"I will," I said.

Finally, he took the stack of folders from me, and I opened the door to let him out. But he was still looking at me with those intense eyes.

"No more than necessary," he said.

"Hey, you said you trusted me," I reminded him.

"I do," he said. Then he reached up to adjust his knit cap before stepping out the door.

The minute I shut it behind him, I was running up the stairs, all the way to the attic, where my 1928 clothes were stored.

CHAPTER 5

When I stepped out of the back door and headed for the orchard at the back of the garden, I was surprised to find it was late afternoon already. I had spent more time with Nick than I thought I had. The story with all the details had been a long one, but on top of that, I tended to lose track of time in the real world when I was looking at things so intently in the world of webs.

That explained all the eggs and toast with butter I had scarfed down. I had been hungry because I had missed lunch.

I looked over all of Brianna's brass instruments arranged throughout the garden first. They hadn't sensed a single thing since I had collapsed the time portal down to the narrowest of wormholes, but I always started with them just to be sure. If anything were trying to break through, I'd want to have some hint of it before I went into the world of threads. Patricia had shown me just how vulnerable I was there. Nothing was the slightest bit off about them, so I went ahead and settled down on the ground in the center of the orchard and fell into a pattern of slow, deep breaths.

I didn't turn my attention to the wormhole. Not at first. Instead, I expanded my awareness out from where I was, looking for signs of other witches. No one was watching me; that I was sure of. The only power I felt was the constant hum of the school itself behind me.

I stretched out further, searching for any sign of magic at all, even if it wasn't directed towards me or the school or the portal. Nothing.

Then, on a whim, I turned my attention across the river to the highway on-ramp that had been the scene of the accident. I had never dwelled in such a place while in the world of webs before; it was a bit dizzying. I could see so many threads whizzing by, a world of stories rushing past me too fast to properly sense. It was like an ocean of white noise I couldn't make sense of.

I forced my mind to focus on the road itself, and then I could catch glimpses of threads that told the story of just this location. I found fragments of stories. I felt the fear of the teenage girl, a new driver in her first fender bender. I sensed the anger of the impatient man who rear-ended her. But these were old stories. Snow had been falling in both of their memories. That was months past.

But I could find nothing newer. There was no sign of anyone cutting away threads, and there was nothing like the rabbit, trying but failing to connect to the world around it. It was as if nothing like Nick had described had ever happened here. Certainly not so recently as he said.

Was he wrong somehow? Or perhaps Debra, so adept at erasing memories, was also capable of implanting false ones?

But could even Patricia fabricate something like the rabbit? And if she did, why?

Nothing made any sense.

I turned my attention back to the portal itself and examined it with such close attention I twice nearly blacked out from forgetting to keep my body breathing. But everything was exactly as it should be.

The answers weren't here. Perhaps I would find more in 1928. With a gesture, I telescoped myself down to a stream of particles that flowed through the narrow neck of the wormhole, reassembling in 1928.

I felt my body putting itself back into shape, but I didn't plunge back into it right away. Instead, I repeated every step I had taken on the other side. I examined the portal, the school, and the world around me as far as I could extend myself, hunting for any sign of magic, any sign of a witch. Any sign of an attack.

But there was nothing. I wasn't going to learn any more here than I had back in the present.

I opened my eyes, pulling my sweater closer around me as a sudden chill set me to shivering. I don't think it was entirely the weather; the moment I tried to take a step, I knew that my day had been more intensively magical than most. I was on the verge of collapsing. I needed food and rest.

I looked up at the school. The lights were shining out of many of the windows, although I couldn't hear anyone moving around inside. If food and rest were truly all I needed, I only had to take a dozen or so steps to find it.

But I needed something more. So I hugged myself a little tighter and bent my head as I focused on putting one foot in front of the other, down the side path to the front yard, then across Summit Avenue.

I shuffled my way down the cobblestones of Maiden Lane, but when I reached the bottom of the wooden stairs up to Edward's door, my energy gave out completely. I reached out for the railing and barely caught it in time to change a fall to my knees into a hurried sitting on the bottom step.

I just needed a minute.

Or so I thought. But after a minute, I had to admit to myself the swooping feeling in my head wasn't letting up at all.

"Edward," I called. I was going to call again, but the blackness that had been building at the edges of my vision was closing in fast. I couldn't feel the step I was sitting on. I couldn't feel anything but the cold.

"Amanda!"

Someone was pulling me up. I cracked open my eyes to see Edward. From his clothes, I guessed he was only now coming home from work. He tried to set me on my feet, but when my knees immediately buckled, he slipped an arm around me instead.

"I need to lie down," I said, blinking hard as the motion of him pulling me around made my vision rock crazily back and forth like I was standing on the deck of a ship crossing the high seas.

"Let's get upstairs first," he said. "Can you walk a little?"

I made a mumble of sound in reply and focused all my attention on my own feet. Stupid feet. My toes kept catching on the edges of the steps, but somehow Edward managed to wrestle me up the narrow staircase and through the door. The apartment was in darkness, but it was only a few steps to the edge of his bed.

My consciousness slipped away for a little bit then. I was vaguely aware of the murmur of Edward's voice, although whether he was speaking to me or someone else, I couldn't tell. Then there was a clatter of pans in his kitchen nook, the smell from the stove as he poked the fire back to life, the harsh bitterness of coffee brewing.

Then even that bit of awareness went away, and I fell into a deep, dreamless sleep.

When I opened my eyes sometime later, I saw the dark of night outside the window. The lamp on Edward's table was glowing warmly, and there was a darker glow from the open grate of the stove. Edward himself had pulled a chair up to the side of the bed and was asleep there now. He had taken off his work coat and rolled up his shirt sleeves, but had not bothered to loosen his tie or even take off his hat.

As if feeling my eyes on him, he woke with a start.

"Amanda," he said, sitting forward to grasp my hand.

"Edward," I said, giving his hand a squeeze.

"Were you attacked? Are we in danger?"

"No, I just overdid it," I said. "I was searching for clues and not paying enough attention to my body back in the real world."

"Clues for what?" Edward asked.

"A boy is missing," I said. "In 2019. Or maybe missing is the wrong word. It's more like he never existed. Only the police officer who helped him and I are aware of his existence, and I never even met him."

"I don't think I follow you," Edward said. "Do you want some coffee?"

"What time is it?" I asked. Edward pulled out his pocket watch and flipped it open. "Just after four."

"Ugh," I said, rubbing at my face. "Yes, coffee would be great. I don't think I'm going to be getting any more sleep, anyway."

"We didn't have an arranged meeting for tonight," he said. He took a crock of butter down from a shelf and added a generous dollop to my coffee.

"I'm sorry if I scared you, just turning up like that," I said.

"I just meant Otto isn't here," he said, handing me the mug of coffee. Then he turned to fix his own, with cream from the icebox and just a sprinkle of sugar.

"Were you talking to him before? I heard voices."

"I spoke to him on the phone. He's busy tonight, but if it's an emergency..."

"No, that's fine," I said, waving a hand as I took a long sip from the mug. At that moment, the bitterness of it was good. It was like a stab to all my senses.

"Did you need something from me, then?" he asked.

"I was checking the time portal for signs of someone using it or tampering with it or straight out attacking it, first back in my time and then here," I said. "As I told you, it was more exhausting than I realized. I didn't know just how much it had taken out of me until I went back into my physical body. The state I was in, I don't think I could've moved myself back to 2019 even if I had wanted to."

"You didn't want to?"

I smiled at him. "You know, I never really want to. I always prefer to be here, with you."

"Do you?"

"You know I do," I said. "Every moment I can possibly be here, I'll be here."

"Until you can't," he said.

"Maybe it never comes to that," I said. "I've been building my power, you know. Maybe there's a way to get this coven out of the way and restore the portal to what it once was."

"That's thirteen witches to get out of the way, Amanda," he said. "And I've seen those witches. I've seen what they can do."

"And you've seen what I can do," I said. "Do you think they're going to win?"

"I don't know what's going to happen," he said. "I just worry about you."

"I can take care of myself," I said.

"But what if the right thing to do is to destroy that time portal entirely? I mean, what if you find out that it's how someone made that boy disappear, and you can't stop them from using it? What if destroying it entirely is the only way to keep everyone safe?"

"Then I'll destroy it," I said. "I know how to do it. I've thought it through many, many times. I'm not going to stand by and let people get hurt."

Edward nodded, but his eyes were gazing deeply into his own coffee mug.

"Hey," I said, shifting to sit on the edge of the bed and set aside my own coffee to put my hands on his. Reluctantly, he looked back up at me. "I'll do what I have to do. I'm not afraid. I know you understand. I know if our roles were reversed, you would do the same. Because you care about people. You care about what happens to this boy, and you've never even seen what he looks like."

He didn't answer right away. Then he swallowed hard before he finally got the words out. "You're right. I would do the same as you. I believe that too. With all my heart. I trust you."

"The thing is, I'm at the school because I have a calling, to protect that portal," I said. "If the portal is gone, so is my calling. There will be nothing left to protect."

"Okay," Edward said, but I could tell that he wasn't following me.

"That means there's no reason I have to be standing in 2019 when I take that portal down," I said. "I could do it from here."

"And then be trapped here forever?" he asked.

I smiled at him. "I don't think I'd describe spending the rest of my natural-born years by your side as being 'trapped.'"

"But you'd be leaving everything behind," he said.

"There's really not much there for me," I said.

"Brianna and Sophie," he said.

"Are my best friends," I agreed. "And I'd miss them. But not half so much as I'd miss you if we were separated. I think that just might kill me."

"Same," Edward said, focused on his coffee again. Then he finished it off in one long swallow. "I guess we better make sure we're not separated, then."

"Exactly," I said. "And hey, the coven has made no move to try to take the portal. Maybe we're worrying over nothing."

"But the boy," Edward said.

"Yes, Jackson. I have to find him," I said, then sighed. "I thought there might be clues here, but there's nothing. If the coven is behind this, I don't know how they're doing it. Or why. I think this just might be a 2019 problem."

"So you're going back there," he said.

"I'll be back tonight, if just to give you an update," I said. "If you do speak to Otto today, see if he's turned up anything."

"I ask him that daily," Edward said. "He insists he can contact you himself if he needs to, through the school, but I ask anyway."

"He's not wrong, but I'm glad you're here too," I said. "And not just for following up on investigations, or letting me hog your bed when I'm under the weather, or bringing me coffee. I told you I've been feeling like I have more magic at my fingertips than ever before."

"I thought that was bonding with your wand?" he said.

"Maybe that's part of it," I said. "But mostly I think it's you. You recharge me. I'm stronger for having you with me."

"I feel the same," he said, then flushed. "I know I'm not a witch, but—"

"I know what you mean," I said. "I know exactly what you mean."

CHAPTER 6

The knocking on the door wasn't particularly startling. It had started as a normal, brisk knock that became more insistent when not answered. Even then, it wasn't a rude pounding. Just someone who suspected the sound of them knocking on the door might have to travel up a few flights of stairs to reach me.

No, what had startled me was that I was sitting up on the parlor sofa with no memory of how I got there. The only thing I knew for sure was that I had been sleeping there for some time.

It was even less comfortable than Edward's sofa. And I wouldn't have thought that possible. But Miss Zenobia's front parlor was decorated for elegance, not comfort.

I got to my feet and nearly spilled to the floor as I discovered too late that I had gone numb from the knees down. That, plus I was still wearing the cloak that hid me from other witches, and the folds of it were twisting around my legs.

I struggled to get the cloak off and throw it down on one of the wing-backed chairs, then stumbled towards the front hall, using every piece of furniture on the way for support. My legs were waking up, with all the pins and needles extra sharp and pointy.

I flung the door open, catching Nick mid knock. The house faced to the west, and the front door was tucked away in the back of a low, shady porch, so no direct sunlight ever reached it. But even the diffuse rays that reached my eyes were too much, and I fell back from the door.

"Amanda?" Nick asked, but didn't wait for an answer. He had seen me covering my eyes and quickly stepped inside, shutting the door behind him. "Are you all right? It looks like you have the mother of all hangovers."

"No," I said, but then realized that was rather what it felt like. "Well, maybe. But from too much magic, not from drinking."

"Did you learn anything?" he asked, but before I could answer, he was talking again. "Never mind that. Do you need anything? Water or something?"

"I'm not dehydrated," I said. "I'll be fine in a minute."

"You've been through this before?" he asked.

"Similar," I said, still rubbing at my forehead. "I was in the world of threads for a long time, both here and in 1928."

"Are you sure you don't want anything?" he asked.

"I smell coffee," I said. "Let's start with that."

Nick walked with me to the kitchen. As I poured out two cups of coffee, the smell of dark roast washed over me, and I had a sudden memory of another cup of less aromatic coffee.

"I was up before four," I said, piecing the memories together. Nick raised an eyebrow but didn't speak. "That was in 1928. I collapsed yesterday but felt all right when I woke up. I had some coffee and came home. I felt perfectly fine until I traveled through the time portal. Wow," I said, as more memories rushed back to my waking mind. "I've gone through that portal dozens of times since I collapsed it down to a wormhole, but for some reason, this time, it really packed a wallop."

"Has something changed? Is it compromised?" he asked.

"No," I said, but in truth, I wasn't sure. I had checked everything out before I had used it to get home, I remembered that. But had I checked it again after arriving in 2019? That I couldn't remember. I set my coffee back down with a sigh. "Wait here."

I went out the back door to the orchard and sat down on the ground. I was afraid my mind would be too muddled, but after a few meditative breaths, I blinked easily into the world of threads.

Nothing appeared out of place. I started to search more deeply, but then reminded myself that this had dug up nothing the last few times I had tried it.

It had also broken my brain a little bit.

Still, I wanted to be sure.

I made an attempt to both stay aware of my physical form and look more closely at the fabric of things around me. That worked about as well as one might expect.

I gave up with another sigh and got up, brushing the dirt from my 1920s skirt before heading back into the house.

"Anything?" Nick asked. He was leaning on the counter where I had left him, but I could smell bread browning in the toaster, and my stomach gave a sudden loud rumble.

"Nothing," I said. "Everything is exactly as it should be in 2019 and 1928 both, and I just don't understand it."

"Maybe they aren't using the portal to do their magic this time," Nick said. "Maybe they found something else, like the wardrobe." The toaster popped, and he turned to put the hot slices on plates and smear them thickly with butter.

"That wardrobe is a very rare piece of magic," I said. "I doubt they could find another. And even if they had, I would have seen it when I was searching for sources of power. It would have glowed so brightly I could see it from Wisconsin. But there was nothing."

"Okay, let's think this through," Nick said, taking the plates over to the table. I picked up my coffee and followed him. He took a bite of his toast, then licked a bit of butter off his thumb before counting off points on his fingers. "We know it isn't the wardrobe, and we know it isn't the portal. You said you're sure it's not another magical object like the wardrobe."

"I didn't even sense another witch directing energy anywhere," I said. Then a sudden thought struck me. "I should find the spot in 2019 that corresponds to where their tower was in 1928."

"Do you know where it is?" he asked.

"About," I said. "I could get one of Otto's maps and bring it here and figure it out easily enough."

"Okay, but what will that tell you?" Nick asked. "You said you searched pretty thoroughly. If something big were happening there, you would have sensed it, right?"

"Probably?" I said with a frown. "That coven is very good at hiding what they're up to. They have witches with a lot of masking and illu-sion-creating powers."

"But you've seen through them before," Nick said. "And they know that."

"What are you saying?" I asked, finally turning my attention to my own toast.

"Well, it's just a thought," Nick said, "but what if they aren't even using magic?"

"How can they remove a boy from existence, from everyone's memories, and not be using magic?" I asked.

"Well, this is just a theory," Nick said. "I don't know much about magic, and I definitely don't understand it. But I have seen *Back to the Future* a couple dozen times."

"What does that have to do with it?" I asked.

"If you were in 1928 and you wanted to change things in 2019, you wouldn't need magic to do it," Nick said. "You could just keep your own parents from meeting."

"Or grandparents," I said. "You're right. It would be so simple."

"But why this boy, though?" Nick asked.

"Maybe it wasn't just him," I said. "Maybe they've been trying things since I collapsed the portal, and this is just the first one I've noticed."

"That's an evil thought," Nick said with a shudder. "How many people are missing, and no one even knows they're gone?"

"But we remember him," I said. "Or rather you do. I never met him."

"There's another thing," Nick said. "His file has disappeared."

"Disappeared?"

"That's what I came over to tell you in the first place. I was looking it over again last night before I went to sleep, but when I woke up this morning, it was gone. I searched everywhere in case I had just misplaced it, but it's really gone."

"The rabbit too?" I asked.

Nick jerked as if something had shocked him, then started patting down his pockets. The growing panic on his face became a look of immense relief as he found it and pulled it out to set it on the table between us. "Maybe you should hold on to it."

"Are you sure?" I asked.

"Yes," he said. "Until you mentioned it, I had forgotten it even existed. It's better that you should have it."

"I might end up needing it," I said, running my fingers over the bare patches at the ends of its floppy ears.

"Amanda, promise me you'll remember him," Nick said, reaching across the table to catch hold of my hands, still clutching the bunny. The anguished look in his eyes stabbed at my heart.

"Of course I will," I said. "You will too."

"I don't want to forget him," Nick said. "But I feel like he's slipping away from me. I'm afraid I'll forget all about him, and I won't even realize that I have. I won't know what I've lost."

"Hey," I said, and now I was the one squeezing his hands. "I'm going to fix this. You've just opened up a whole other line of investigation for me to work on. I don't think I'd ever have thought to look for a nonmagical answer to what's happening. But now that you've said it, it just fits, doesn't it?"

"But we don't have a photograph to watch him slowly fade away or reappear," Nick said. "We won't know whether we're succeeding or failing."

"We don't need a photograph," I said. "We just need to find out who he is. Who his parents and grandparents were. Then I can find out what part of his family tree just got severed."

"What if someone was killed?" Nick asked.

"I don't know," I admitted. "I doubt I could fix that. But I don't think it's too likely. The witches are trying to keep a low profile. And why kill someone when just keeping two people from meeting would do the trick?"

"I hope you're right," Nick said. "But he had disappeared from all official records even before I came to see you the first time. I know he was an orphan, and the first check for living relatives after his parents died didn't turn up any. And his last name is Smith."

"I can see why you find that discouraging," I said, picking up the rabbit again. "But maybe we don't need official records."

"The rabbit can tell you?" Nick asked.

"Hopefully," I said.

"But you looked at it before and didn't find anything useful, did you?"

"Not with my usual magic, no," I said. "But there are other spells I can try. I'm sure Brianna knows a dozen."

"Are you going to call her home?" he asked.

"No, not yet," I said. "That's a last resort, and we're not there yet."

"Okay," Nick said, and I could tell he was working hard to have faith in me.

"Hey, all the spells she knows? They're all in the books upstairs. She found them there. I can find them too."

"Of course you can," he said. Then he finished off his coffee in one long swallow. "I should go. I blew off all my morning classes, but I have a test I'm about to be late for that I really can't miss."

"I'll text you if I learn anything," I said.

"I just hope it's good news, and that I'll still know what you're talking about when you tell me," he said.

"If it's good news, you will," I said.

After closing the door behind Nick, I went back into the parlor to retrieve the cloak. It was a good thing I was still dressed for 1928, if a bit mussed from twice sleeping in those clothes.

Rabbit clutched tightly in my hand, I threaded myself back through the wormhole to the past. The rabbit wasn't connected to anything in 2019, but it wanted to be. I had seen its long threads winding through everything. Perhaps in 1928, those connections were still intact. Perhaps they could lead me to the lost boy's ancestors.

If not, I would have to do the one thing I dreaded more than anything else.

I would have to force myself to go into that library and attempt to understand Brianna's books.

CHAPTER 7

I was back in 1928, and still there was no sign of the coven of witches. No one was watching the charm school. No one was trying to access the portal.

I looked down at the rabbit in my hand but decided I wanted to be somewhere it was safe to collapse before I tried looking at its threads. I felt fine, but I had felt fine twice before.

It was just past noon, and Edward was out at work when I let myself into his place. I took off the cloak and hung it on the hook by the door, then crossed the room to the table that was still strewn with maps. Some of them were drawn by hand, some torn out of map books or purchased downtown. I found the most up to date one that Otto had marked with the locations of sewer lines and bootlegging tunnels. The location of the witches' tower was traced in heavy red wax pencil lines. I folded it up and stuffed it in my pocket.

Then I settled on the couch, rabbit in hand, and shifted my awareness to the world of threads.

At first, the rabbit looked much the same as it had in 2019, not quite part of the world around it. I suppose I should have expected that. Why would it be more connected to this world, long before it had even been made?

But I reminded myself that what I was interested in wasn't the rabbit itself. I wasn't trying to find the origin of the cotton that stuffed its belly or the thread that traced out its remaining eye and whiskers. No, what I wanted was to find the source of the love that had been infused into it over the years of a boy's childhood.

Maybe reading Brianna's books would have been the easier task.

But I wasn't ready to give up just yet. I just had to try something new. I focused more on my physical body, and specifically on the way that rabbit felt resting in my hands. I was already holding onto the threads that kept my lungs breathing and my heart beating. Now I added in a few more, to keep my fingers stroking those worn ears.

Then I looked deeper inside the rabbit, past the threads that formed the cotton stuffing and plush exterior, to the smaller but brighter threads that were a boy's love of his special toy.

I wasn't sure I was doing it. Those threads were so tiny the thought occurred to me that I was either imagining them or had created them myself just by touching the rabbit.

When the entire world around me lit up at once, that second theory started sounding a lot more plausible. Then I realized that none of that brightness was coming from me. It wasn't even touching me. The rabbit had a bond with the world around us that didn't include me.

But was it the world around us, or just the apartment?

I grabbed more of my body's threads, walking myself out the door and down the steps, my physical hands still stroking the rabbit's ears.

It was a good thing no one was around in the middle of the day on sleepy Maiden Lane. My marionette skills weren't great, and my body was lurching around like a zombie.

I stopped when I reached the cobblestones, partly to take a look around, but mostly because it was a minor miracle I had made it down the steps without my body taking a nasty tumble and I needed a moment to regroup.

The light that surrounded the rabbit and me was fainter here. I looked back up at the apartment and saw that it was still glowing as brightly as before.

What did this mean? Had the witches attempted to attack Edward and somehow eliminated this boy instead? But how?

Also, being collateral damage from an attack on Edward didn't fit the *Back to the Future* theory. I needed to know more.

I focused on keeping my fingers stroking the rabbit's ears and gazing into its heart until something else caught my eye. A single thread, brighter than the rest, so fine I could barely see it, but so long I couldn't see where it ended.

I left my body there at the bottom of the stairs and followed that thread. It was pointing straight towards Summit Avenue, and a lurching zombie crossing that busy street would draw too much attention. Hopefully, no one passed by and wondered why a grown woman was standing at the bottom of the stairs, stroking a stuffed rabbit's ears with a blank look on her face.

The thread was so small I nearly lost sight of it more than once. It was slow going and required so much focus on the tiny thread that I wasn't paying attention to the rest of the world around me.

Then I lost the thread entirely. I was about to backtrack and try to catch it again when I realized there was a bright glow right in front of me.

The charm school.

Only the thread hadn't been leading there. It had been going in a direction that would take it just past it. To Coco's house.

I lurched back into my own body, sucking in a great lungful of air that wasn't enough to fight the wave of dizziness. I sat down hard on the bottom step and rested my head on the railing.

The glow from the charm school had only been its usual magic-infused form. It hadn't been connected to the rabbit, or at least I didn't think so.

But that thread had been running to Coco's house. The thread had been so attenuated it had nearly ceased to exist in several places. The house itself hadn't been filled with light, as Edward's apartment had. Was that because the person it connected with was no longer alive?

Was the rabbit's only real connection to this world Ivy, who had died on New Year's Eve?

I looked up at Edward's door at the top of the stairs. With just my mundane vision, there was nothing special to see there. But the entire space had glowed before. What did that mean?

I pushed myself onto my feet and climbed the steps to the apartment. My mind was in a whirl, but at least my body wasn't failing me this time.

That was good. Because there was no time for epic midday naps now, no matter how badly I might need one.

I picked up Edward's phone and called Otto. I expected he'd be sleeping, and I would have to convince his young protégé, Benny, to wake him up, but it was Otto himself that picked up the line.

"It's Amanda," I said after the grunt of sound that probably hadn't been "hello."

"Trouble?" he asked, suddenly wide awake.

"Nothing dire," I said. "I need a ride. Can you send Benny with the car?"

"You're at Edward's?" he guessed.

"Yes," I said.

"I'll be there in five minutes," he said, then hung up before I could tell him not to lose any sleep on my account.

Four minutes later, I could hear him barreling up the narrow lane. I was already cloaked with the rabbit in my hand, ready to run down to meet him.

I realized I was paranoid that if I put that rabbit away in a pocket that I would forget it existed, just as Nick had. Or maybe that wasn't paranoia. Maybe I really would.

"Where to?" Otto asked as I slid into the seat next to him.

"Edward's work first," I said. "I don't need to see him; I just need to check something."

Otto nodded and put the car in gear. Then he took a drink from a thermos, and I suspected that when more of that coffee was inside of him, he'd have more questions for me.

A few minutes later, he pulled up to a curb outside a tall brick building downtown.

"He's in there," he said, pointing with his chin. "Third floor. Do you need to know which window?"

"No, I've got it from here," I said and moved to the world of threads.

I don't know what I had been hoping for exactly, but my heart sank when I saw the thread running from the rabbit up to the third floor of that building. The thread's light was pulsing, each pulse ever so slightly less bright than the one before. It wasn't trying to connect to a dead person, and yet even with the person on the other end alive, the connection was dying.

I opened my eyes with a sigh.

"Is he all right?" Otto asked.

"Edward? He's fine," I said.

"What's with the rabbit?"

I bet that thermos was empty now.

"I don't know exactly," I said.

"You're being waffly," Otto said.

"It's hard to explain," I said.

"So don't explain it," he said with a shrug. "Just tell me why you look like someone just pulled the carpet out from under you."

"This rabbit belongs to a little boy in 2019 who seems to have been erased from existence. For all I know, I'm the only one who remembers him now, and I never even met him."

"And what does that have to do with Edward?"

"Edward and Ivy," I said, and found myself stroking the rabbit's ears again. Even worn as they were, it was still a comfort. "I think maybe they were supposed to get married and have kids. And grandkids. And eventually this kid."

"But Ivy died months ago," Otto said.

"The coven might have been driving Charlotte to that end more than we thought at the time," I said. "They denied it. They said it was just fate, but I'm starting to think it was intentional."

"Just to get rid of this kid decades later?" Otto asked.

"Maybe," I said.

"Why? Who's this kid? Is he going to be president someday or something?"

"I don't know," I said. "I'm working on it."

"You think it's all about you," he guessed.

"Can you blame me?" I shot back, annoyed. Then I took a deep breath. "Can you drive by the tower? I want to see if anything from the rabbit connects to them."

"Is it worth the risk?" he asked.

"There's no risk unless they know we're there," I said, straightening the folds of my cloak around me. He just kept giving me the side-eye until I said, "yes, it's worth the risk. It's a kid."

"You're the boss," he said and pulled away from the curb.

He didn't park by the tower, but I didn't need him to. He just kept driving around and around the block we knew contained that tower while I examined the threads.

The rabbit wasn't connected to anything around us.

And as hard as I tried, I couldn't sense the tower I knew still had to be there.

But was that true? Did it have to be there? The coven had created it with magic without anyone knowing. Surely they could dismantle it just as covertly.

But no. It didn't make sense for them to just disappear. They hadn't got what they wanted yet, and they'd worked too long and hard to get it. They wouldn't just give up.

"Nothing?" Otto said as I came back into my body and opened my eyes.

"No," I said. "I really think it's time to just call them out."

"Not on your own, you don't," Otto said. "Call the others back first."

"No, it's too soon for that," I said.

"Your and Edward's days of wine and roses are going to end, you know," he said.

"I'm not talking about that," I said, my cheeks heating. Leave it to Otto to just know how much I'd been hiding about how little Brianna and Sophie knew about my activities.

"Sure you're not," he said.

"I'm not," I said. "They left town for a reason, you know."

"Is that adding up to anything, then?" he asked.

"Maybe," I said.

"I think you need to call them back," he said.

"Not yet," I said, then sighed. "Look, I'll be talking to them again tomorrow morning. The three of us will decide then, okay? There's more going on in 2019 than you know."

"Fair enough," Otto said. "Anywhere else you need to go?"

"No, back to the school is fine," I said. Then I put the rabbit in my sweater pocket.

I told myself there was no way I would forget about Jackson, not after all the work I had put in trying to find traces of him in two eras.

But a smaller, more honest voice was whispering that maybe I wanted to forget. Would that be so bad? It's not like I could do anything about Ivy being dead now. I couldn't go any further back into the past than where I was now.

It was more like having two presents than actually having the power to travel through time.

But I didn't like what that voice was saying.

I took the rabbit back out of my pocket and held it in my hands all the way back to the charm school, and from there back to 2019.

CHAPTER 8

I was the first one to log in to the conference call in the morning. I fidgeted in the chair, tapping the edge of the desk with what I thought was a pen, but turned out to be my wand. I quickly put that away, then decided the safest thing to do was to go ahead and find a pen to tap with.

I hadn't even had any coffee yet.

I heard the tone and looked up to see Sophie settling into her own chair. Her expression was the usual coolly implacable look she always had, but something was off. Not her hair; her hair was as always totally on point.

Then I saw it.

"What happened?" I asked.

Her eyes widened. "What do you mean?"

"You do realize you're covered in mud," I said. "Your shoulders are covered in mud. How did your shoulders get covered in mud?"

Sophie glanced down and made a face, then took out her wand and, with a single sweeping motion, cleaned herself up.

I wasn't the only one who had been deepening the bond with my wand.

"What happened?" I asked again.

"It's not important," she said with a dismissive wave. "We've had a lot of rain lately, and rain makes mud. I was out running, and I slipped. And that's the end of the epic tale of how Sophie DuBois got dirty."

I wasn't sure I bought it. I had known Brianna to jog on occasion, and I liked long walks myself, but Sophie was more of an exercise indoors type of girl.

"Were you running after someone? Or away from?" I asked.

"Sort of both," she said. "But it turned out to just be a pack of kids, so no big deal."

"Did you get in contact with any of the local covens, then?" I asked.

"No," Sophie said. "I can tell they're watching me everywhere I go, but no one is letting me get close. They don't trust me."

"Because of your mother?"

"Maybe?" Sophie said. "Since no one will talk to me, I don't really know. There might not be much more I can do here on my own. Not without doing something desperate. Any news on your end?"

But before I could answer, a window with Brianna's face popped open on my screen.

"Hey," she said.

"Hey yourself," I said. "You sound down. Everything all right?"

"I'm just tired," she said.

Through the magic of computer cameras, Sophie and I exchanged a look. Neither of us was exactly sure when Brianna slept. We both suspected she let entire nights go by without so much as a catnap.

But we'd never heard her complain of being tired before.

"Are you taking care of yourself?" Sophie asked.

"That's a strange question," Brianna said.

"Do you have someone to make sure you're eating at least a meal a day and hopefully stepping away from your books for a little fresh air once in a while?" I asked.

"Oh," she said. "Yeah, I guess you guys *do* do that. And Mr. Trevor."

"Does Boston have anything like a Mr. Trevor?" I asked.

"No," she said, and actually yawned. "I had a sandwich. A turkey and cheese thing on toasted cranberry bread."

"Just now?" I asked.

Brianna scrunched up her face. "Yesterday, maybe? But it was later in the day. I think."

"Let me guess," Sophie said, leaning forward into her camera. "This hidden library you found is underground somewhere, and you've been spending all your time there. Without clocks or your cellphone or anything to measure the passage of time."

"You should see the things I've found here, though!" Brianna said.

"What about the meeting?" I interrupted before Brianna could start enthusing over old books. "How did that go?"

"I do have some things to share with you on that," she said, taking out her little notebook and turning the pages. "I'm not sure I believe all of it, though. At least, I want to double-check as much as I can here before I come home."

"What did she say?" I asked.

"I don't want to say," Brianna said. "Not until I double-check some things. If it's true, it's huge. But I don't think it's true."

"Why don't you just tell us, and we can be the judge?" Sophie asked.

"No, it's just..." Brianna broke off, rubbing at her face. "Trust me?"

"Of course we trust you," I said. Sophie still looked skeptical, but gave a little nod.

"We should plan for another call tomorrow," Brianna said. "I'll have something to share by then. I have everything right here that I need to verify if what she told me is even possible."

"I was just telling Amanda that I think I've done all I can here in New Orleans," Sophie said to Brianna. I slumped back in my chair and started tapping with the pen again.

They were going to want to come home soon. It was time. Only I hadn't yet figured out how to explain to them about the change in my relationship with Edward. I had absolutely no intention of carrying on in secret with my frequent visits to 1928 once they were back, but I also had no intention of giving them up.

I was going to have to tell them. And they were going to argue against it. It was going to be a heavy, awkward confrontation, and there was no way to get around it.

But maybe it was time to stop delaying it.

"Amanda?" Sophie said, catching my attention.

"Sorry, what?" I asked.

"We were just asking how the journal work was progressing?" she asked.

"I wouldn't really call it progress," I said with a sigh. "It's slow going, and I haven't learned anything new in the little bit I've slogged through."

"It always was a long shot," Brianna said, sounding more depressed than ever.

"Maybe you can get more out of it than I have when you get back," I said.

"Is it time to come back?" Brianna asked.

"Not if you still had things to do in Boston," I said. "There's nothing major going on here."

"I've definitely hit a dead end," Sophie said. "Even if anyone in a coven here knows anything about what happened to my mother or to yours, they're never going to tell me about it. I might as well come home."

"If you're sure," I said. "Nick is checking in with the P.I. he hired. He's supposed to be texting when he knows anything, but I'm sure I'll see him this afternoon after he's done with classes. We're working on another thing together, so I know he'll stop by."

Brianna and Sophie were both looking at me with confusion written across their faces.

"What?" I asked. "Oh, I hadn't explained about that case. Don't worry about it. I'll bring you up to speed as soon as you're home. In the meantime, Nick and I have got it in hand. Really, no worries."

The confusion on Brianna's face deepened, and she bent her head to start paging back through her little notebook. I could see her mumbling to herself as she scanned the pages. Since she didn't know what I was talking about, I figured she had gone off on a tangent. It wouldn't be the first time Brianna hadn't been listening to me talk.

But Sophie was still giving me a confused look, and I knew she had been listening.

"What is it?" I asked her.

Her eyes searched my face like she was trying to tell if I were joking or not. Finally, she asked, "Amanda, who's Nick?"

Now I was the one trying to figure out if she was joking. "Hey, you promised to stop teasing me about these things," I said.

Sophie pondered that for a moment. "I promised to stop teasing about Edward," she said.

"And Nick," I said. "Why are you pretending not to know Nick?"

"Amanda, I'm not pretending anything," Sophie said.

The moment I believed her, that she wasn't teasing me or making some unfunny joke, it was like the floor had fallen away beneath me. My stomach lurched like I had just dropped through a trapdoor and I was falling down, down, forever down.

I lunged forward and caught the edge of the desk. Then I looked straight at Sophie, who was clearly not joking.

"Nick Larson," I said, my mouth suddenly dry. "He lives in the condo next door with his grandfather. I met him the day I came to St. Paul. He helped us with the police after we found Cynthia's body, and also after we found Mrs. Olson's body. He brought me back to the school after Mina Fox tried to poison me. I was visiting him and his grandfather when I found the enchanted wardrobe and the dead gangster."

I watched her face after each detail I added, but her usual aloof poker face was back, and I didn't know if she thought I was lying or crazy or what. "Those things all happened," I said.

"They happened," Sophie agreed. "But the only common thread in them was you. The only cop those two murder scenes had in common was Nelson Fisher. He was perfectly professional, but not particularly friendly. I don't remember ever meeting any Nick Larson."

I put my face in my hands and clutched at my hair. The pain did nothing to clear my head or abate the falling feeling.

Was this happening? Was this really happening? Had he disappeared too? How? Why?

I looked up and saw Brianna closing her book and looking up into the camera.

"Brianna?" I asked. "Do you remember Nick? You must've recorded him in your book. You kept all the details of our investigations in there."

"I did," she said, shifting uncomfortably in her chair. "But Sophie's right. There is no Nick Larson in my notes. There isn't a common element among all those cases except us. Nelson Fisher was the officer in charge of the investigations in the present."

"The wardrobe?" I asked.

"You sensed that from the house," Sophie said.

"Then who saved me from Mina Fox?" I asked.

"You brought yourself home," Sophie said.

Brianna nodded. "We don't know how you did it. Some burst of magical power or something. When you finally recovered, you didn't remember what happened after you trapped Mina in the crystal ball."

"It was Nick," I said. "I would've died if he hadn't been there."

"Maybe we should come home," Sophie said, then at the pained expression on Brianna's face hastily added, "or at least I should."

But I couldn't handle any more of that conversation. I had to find out if Nick really had been erased from the world. Maybe they were affected first because they were so far away. Maybe I still had time?

I made a quick search of the house, but there was no sign of Mr. Trevor. He liked to walk around the neighborhood first thing in the morning, I reminded myself. Surely that was where he was, and he would be home soon.

But the sudden fear that anyone I wasn't directly looking at might just disappear without a trace at any moment was a hard one to shake.

I still remembered Nick. That had to mean something.

And if there was anyone who would remember him better than I, it was his grandfather.

The moment that thought struck me, I ran out of the house to the condo building next door.

CHAPTER 9

The sun was not yet high enough in the sky to warm the remains of the cold night air, especially along our sidewalk that was shaded by trees and both the school and the condo building. I wished I had grabbed a jacket before dashing out of the door.

I ran up the concrete steps and pressed the buzzer for his grandfather's apartment. Another wave of panic tried to overwhelm me, but I fought it back, moving my finger from the buzzer to find the name next to the apartment number was still Larson.

When there was no answer after the third time I rang, I dug my phone out of my cardigan pocket. I scrolled through my contact list, but Nick's name wasn't there. I checked my texts, then all my call logs, even my email. But there was nothing to or from Nick.

I turned and sat down on the ice-cold concrete steps. The urge to cry was strong, but that wouldn't help anybody. In a burst of desperation, I tried putting his name in my search engine, but the world was full of Nick Larsons, and none of them looked familiar.

Finally, I put my phone away and felt something soft in the bottom of my cardigan pocket. I pulled a small plush rabbit, no larger than the palm of my hand, with worn floppy ears and a missing eye. I had kept no toys from my own childhood, so why did this one look so familiar? And why was it in my pocket?

I touched the place where the tips of the ears had been stroked so many times the plush was worn off the coarser fabric and felt a jolt of memory. This was Jackson Smith's toy rabbit. The only thing left of him in the entire world.

I had nearly forgotten him. No, scratch that. For some stretch of time, I really had forgotten him. Even now, I couldn't summon the memory of his face. Just his eyes. Something familiar about those eyes... but this time, no matter how long I waited, no burst of memory came.

He reminded me of someone, but I couldn't place who. Perhaps if I calmed my mind with meditation, the answer would come. But that wasn't likely to happen sitting on this concrete stoop, its icy coldness seeping into my very bones.

Then another thought struck me. Had Nick left anything behind?

I was trying to think of anything Nick might have given me or left behind at the charm school by mistake when I heard the sound of dog nails on the sidewalk and looked up to see Nick's grandfather with a newspaper in one hand and Finnegan's leash in the other.

I stood up, but had no idea what to say. If he had forgotten Nick, how would he even know who I was?

"Why, good morning, Miss Clarke," he said as he tucked the newspaper under his arm to fish his keys out of his pocket. "Always lovely to see you."

"You have no idea how good it is to see you," I said. He raised an eyebrow in mock alarm, but his eyes were twinkling.

"Indeed? What can I do for you?" he asked. "Are you still researching the history of this plot of land? Something about an explosion in the 60s I believe?"

"That, and more recent events," I said. "But actually, what I came to talk to you about now is Nick."

"Nick," he repeated as he pulled the door open, then wrestled with getting his key back out of the lock.

"Yes, Nick," I said. "You remember Nick?" I didn't say "Nick Larson" or "Nick, your grandson" because what if he didn't remember Nick? It would only be upsetting for me to claim he had a grandson he didn't remember. Even if I could put all this back to rights somehow and he would never remember our conversation, I just couldn't do that to him.

But I could tell he knew how important his answer was to me. He took a long time answering, like he was being very sure, before he said, "I'm sorry. I'm not sure I've met anyone named Nick. Is this a friend of yours?"

"Yes, a friend," I said, and that feeling of plummeting forever down through the earth was rushing through me again. "I thought I introduced you once, but now that I think about it, I don't think I did. I'm sorry to have bothered you."

"Young lady, you're never a bother," he said. "Best of luck finding your friend."

"Thanks," I said, and gave Finnegan a half-hearted pat on the head before going back down the steps towards the charm school.

I went to my room and hunted around, but the only thing I had from Nick was the rabbit, which wasn't even his. All our communications were gone from my phone and my computer as if they had never existed.

Just the day before, we had questioned whether the witches had erased others in their attempt to get to someone I knew. They must not have realized that they had succeeded with the boy Jackson when they targeted Nick.

Or they knew and didn't care, because the plan had always been to remove as many people as possible. Perhaps everyone I knew.

Perhaps they could even erase people in Iowa, like my foster grandparents, the Schneidermans.

That thought brought the panic back, but all their letters were just where they should be tucked into the drawer of my nightstand.

Still, Jackson disappearing had been a warning, and I hadn't heeded it. And because of that, Nick was gone.

I went back downstairs to the library, expecting to have to send texts to get the others back on their computers, but they were both still on the line. They looked up with palpable relief when I got within range of the camera.

"Amanda?" Sophie asked with deep concern.

"You have to come back," I said, my words garbled by the enormous lump in my throat. I swallowed a few times and tried again. "I need you to come back."

"Is something happening with the portal?" Brianna asked.

"It's the coven, but I don't think they're using the portal," I said. "Nick and I… Okay, I better back up. I know you don't remember Nick, but I promise both of you he's real. He is studying to be a police officer, and he's helped us with some of our investigations. He and I were working together to find information on our mothers, from after they disappeared."

"That part rings a bell," Sophie said. "I remember you were working with… someone."

Brianna was listening intently to both of us, but didn't say a word.

"Good," I said. "That's something, I guess. So anyway, Nick was doing a ride-along with another police officer when they were called to the scene of a car accident. The couple in the front seat was dead on the scene, but the little boy in the back seat was unharmed. Nick sat with him and talked with him until he was taken to a foster family. That was a few days ago. When he went back to the foster home to see how the kid was doing the next morning, no one knew who or what he was talking about."

"You suspect memory magic?" Brianna asked.

"I did at first," I said. "But it wasn't the same as when Evanora or Debra or whoever in the coven took that wardrobe out of the evidence room and wiped the minds of every officer who had seen it or the body. You guys remember that part, right?"

They both nodded.

"Good," I said. "Since Nick was the only one who remembered any of it, I was afraid you might have forgotten."

"You think it's another witch? Or another coven maybe?" Sophie asked.

"I checked for everything I could think of," I said. "The wardrobe is warded as tightly as ever. The portal is still down to the narrowest of wormholes. No one can use either without me seeing signs of it. Then I checked for general magical activity, both here and in the past. Nothing."

"So what's going on?" Sophie asked.

"Well, Nick thought it might be like that movie *Back to the Future*," I said. "If the coven in 1928 can stop people from our past from ever meeting, people who were supposed to have descendants into our present, they can effectively erase people we know."

"But why would they do that?" Brianna asked.

"To get my attention?" I said. "And it's working. Oh boy, is it working."

"That's a big leap," Sophie said.

"You don't understand," I said. "If you remembered Nick, you would. I promise you, anyone who tried to get rid of Nick would know I would come after them."

"I don't doubt you mean it," Sophie said. "I can see you're angry. But you have to sit tight. If you're right and they're trying to draw you out, it's a good bet they are doing it now because they know you're alone."

"Don't do anything without us, Amanda," Brianna said sternly.

"I won't, but I can only wait so long," I said.

"I'm on my way," Sophie said. "There's nothing more I can do here, anyway. And if this Nick person was investigating our mothers, I definitely want to talk with him."

"Maybe that's why they targeted him," Brianna said. "Maybe they knew he was close to something."

"Maybe," I said, but my gut told me this strike was meant to be a lot more personal.

"Okay, I'm booking a flight now," Sophie said, the sound of her fingers rapping on a keyboard on the other side of the country rattling my speakers. "I'll be there by late afternoon. Swear to me you're going to wait until I get there to do anything."

"I swear," I said.

"Anything," Sophie said, drawing out every syllable. "No going back to 1928 just to peek around. You stay put."

I almost blew my own cover by saying she sounded just like Otto. Instead, I just nodded my head.

"Brianna?" Sophie asked.

"I wanted to check..." but she trailed off, looking at something off-camera. Then she nodded. "I'll just bring what I have and explain it all when we're all in the same room."

"Today?" I asked.

"Tonight," she said. "Late."

"And until then, you wait," Sophie said.

"I'll wait," I said, hating the sullen sound even I could hear in my voice. "Be quick."

We disconnected but, having been left with nothing useful to do, I just paced the library, fuming. My hand inside my sweater pocket was still clutching the rabbit, my thumb rubbing over and over the same worn patch of plush at the tips of its ears. Like it was some sort of prayer bead or something.

It was only a toy, and yet still I found it calming. Because as long as I had it, as long as I could still touch it and feel its fur, I still had a piece of Jackson and Nick both with me.

But it was such a small piece.

CHAPTER 10

$\mathcal{I}$ begged off going with Mr. Trevor to the airport to pick up Sophie and Brianna. I told him I had too much work to do, and even went to the library with the intention of getting back to decoding Miss Zenobia's journal. But after staring blankly at the open page for the better part of an hour, I had to admit I wasn't accomplishing anything. Even if I were hard at work, it would be too little too late.

I would just have to admit that, whatever I had said to the contrary, I had not, in fact, put in much of an effort. But I was pretty sure after I told them about my daily trips back to 1928, any frustration they had with me about the journal thing was going to be put on the back burner.

Having nothing else I could even pretend to be doing, I went out to the front porch and bypassed the chairs and porch swing in favor of just sitting on the stoop.

Being the middle of April now, the sun didn't set until eight in the evening, but all the shade from the trees not yet in bud made it still quite chilly. I pulled up the hood of my sweatshirt and pulled my hands deeper into the sleeves, but opted not to go back in. I guess I felt like I needed to do a little penance.

The third time I caught myself watching for people on the sidewalk rather than for Mr. Trevor's town car, I realized I was watching for Nick and Finnegan to come by on their afternoon jog. Only that wasn't going to happen in this world with no Nick in it.

How was I going to fix this?

I would have to go back to 1928 for sure. Or rather, the three of us would have to. But it would be complicated. I had never told Edward or Otto about Nick. There had been no reason to.

Actually, given that Sophie and Brianna didn't remember Nick, maybe that wouldn't be a problem. He could be just a part of the Jackson investigation.

But then, when I got there, what was I going to do? When talking to Brianna and Sophie on the conference call, I hadn't seen past my anger and fierce desire to take the fight straight to the coven. Now, with cooler blood, I could see that maybe there were a few things to look into first. I had nothing of his to follow the threads of like with Jackson's rabbit, but I had something better.

A living relative.

Just then, I heard the sounds of a dog's heavy paws striking the pavement and saw Nick's grandfather walking Finnegan down the sidewalk. Just as if I had summoned him.

"Good afternoon, Miss Clarke," he said when he saw me getting to my feet. "Don't you find it cold, always sitting outside in this weather?"

"I don't mind," I said, resisting the urge to stomp my feet and get the blood flowing. "My friends are on their way home today."

"They've been gone for quite some time, haven't they?" he asked.

"About two months," I said. "Mr. Larson, can I ask you some personal questions?"

"Well, that depends," he said. "How personal?"

"Just your ancestry," I said. "Your family is from Chippewa Falls in Wisconsin, right?"

"Yes, that's correct," he said. He seemed surprised I knew that. But then, without going over to his place to meet him at Nick's request, what opportunity would we have had for those sorts of conversations? It seems he only knew me in regard to my research into the history of the charm school and of the various homes that resided next to it at one time or another.

But now I was going to have to fish a fact out of my brain that I knew I had known at some point. He had talked a lot about his late wife, Nick's grandmother, that evening I had been over for dinner. She had also been from Chippewa Falls. But I could scarcely ask him if he had ever known a Rosemary Larson. What had been her maiden name?

"Schmidt!" I all but shouted.

"Pardon me?" he asked.

"Do you know a Rosemary Schmidt?" I asked. "She would have been about your age, same class at high school, I think. Her family's house was just behind yours. Your backyards were divided by a fence."

"Rosemary Schmidt," he repeated as he dug through his memory. "I remember a Mr. Schmidt, about my father's age, who owned the house behind ours. He didn't have any children, though. Never married that I ever heard of. Always kept to himself. I'm sorry; I don't think I can help you."

So Nick's grandmother's parents had never met. Interesting. But I needed more.

"Maybe you still can," I said. "Do you know anyone still in Chippewa Falls who could help me with a little research?"

"About Mr. Schmidt?" he asked, frowning.

"His personal history, I guess. Perhaps his younger days," I said. "Maybe it's a crazy thing to ask, but you did live behind him."

"I do have a very nosy sister who works at the library there," he said. "If anyone would know, it would be her."

"Would you ask her to look into it for me?" I asked. "I think there must have been someone in his younger days, someone he fancied that never fancied him back. I'm trying to find her name."

"Rosemary?" he ventured.

"Probably not," I admitted. "Don't tell her that name. I don't want to skew her research."

"Research," he laughed. "That's what we're calling decades-old gossip now?"

"Let me give you my email address," I said, digging in my pockets for a scrap of paper. I found my little notebook, a gift from Brianna that I didn't use as often as I should. I tore out a blank sheet and wrote my email address on it. "Anything she can find out for me would be great. I really appreciate it."

"No problem at all, Miss Clarke," he said, folding the page carefully and tucking it into his vest pocket. "And if I'm not mistaken, that would be Mr. Trevor with your friends now. Enjoy your reunion."

"Thanks, have a good evening," I said.

Then I turned my attention to the approaching town car. I had a sudden flashback to the day I had returned from packing up my things in Iowa. I had only been gone for a few days, but Sophie and Brianna had rushed out to greet me with such fervor I had thought they were attacking me.

That was probably why I just hovered on the front walk, not going back to the porch but not going out to the curb, either. That, and just the awkwardness of it all.

Sophie and Brianna climbed out of the car and waved as Mr. Trevor pulled away to drive around the block to his garage. Then they came up the walk towards me.

"Who was that you were talking to?" Sophie asked.

"You don't remember him either?" I asked. But maybe that made sense; I was the only one who had ever met him. "That was Nick's grandfather. He doesn't remember Nick either, but he might know someone who can point us in some sort of direction. We can figure out where it all went wrong in 1928, or at least I hope we can."

"Oh, good," Brianna said. "I like that plan. That's much better than the going in guns blazing plan."

"Or wands blazing," Sophie said. "It's freezing out here. Let's go up to the library and catch up."

"How are the kitties?" Brianna asked as we crossed the threshold.

"They've been missing you," I said.

And indeed, the moment we gathered around Brianna's table in the center of the library, all three cats emerged from the shadows. First, they all mobbed Brianna, demanding her attention even as her eyes were already sweeping around the shelves as if checking in on her book friends. But once we were all sitting in our customary places, the cats each went to their preferred lap to curl up and accept pets.

"I haven't done much with Miss Zenobia's journal," I said, perhaps too forcefully to judge by the startled looks on their faces. "I tried." No, that was a lie. "I tried to try? It was just too much work for too little reward, I guess."

"You told us you were working on it," Sophie said.

"Yeah. Sorry."

Brianna frowned. She started to get up, but the cat in her lap objected. Instead, she took out her wand, summoning the journal, as well as her notes and my notebook. They all flew around the bookshelves from the back of the library to settle neatly on the table in front of her.

"This isn't much," she said, her frown deepening.

"I know," I said. "I don't have an excuse. I should've buckled down, but I didn't."

"Maybe you're right, and it isn't worth the effort," Sophie said diplomatically.

"I can finish it," Brianna said, but that newfound weariness was back in her voice.

"No, if you have other things to work on, I can get back at it," I said.

"No, actually, I have another option," she said. "I have people who can help. Actually, I need to call them quick, anyway. Hold on." Jones again protested, but this time she was undeterred. She set him gently back down on her chair, then went closer to the windows overlooking Summit Avenue before dialing her phone.

I pulled out my own phone and saw I had gotten an email from Nick's grandfather rather formally introducing me to his sister, and then another from his sister asking for more details. She seemed eager to help, and I explained what I needed as briefly as I could. I was just finishing up as Brianna came back to the table.

"One of my people can help with the journal," she said as she picked up Jones and settle back into her chair.

"How?" Sophie asked.

"I brought something with me in my trunk," she said. "It's like a magical mailbox, I guess, keeping me connected to the library in Boston. It'll be a tight fit, but I should be able to get the journal in there. Then the whole team can work on it. We'll have a translation in no time."

"You're going to explain this team of people thing?" Sophie asked.

"Not now," Brianna said. "We worked together to uncover the library, and I trust them, but there's no short way to explain all that now. We have work to do."

"Yes, Nick and Jackson have to come first," I said.

Sophie turned to look at me. "So you weren't working on the translations? Fine. But what else have you been doing all this time that you haven't been telling us?"

This was it. This was the perfect moment to confess. But when I opened my mouth, nothing came out.

I wished I could say it was another one of those compulsions I've had in the past guiding my actions to some unforeseen outcome. But I knew that wasn't it. I just wasn't ready for my friends to start putting roadblocks in the way of me seeing Edward. No matter how reasonable those roadblocks were.

"I've been working with my wand," I said. Which was also true, if not the whole truth. "I've made a lot of progress."

"That *is* good news," Sophie said. "I've been working on things as well. I can do lightning attacks now."

"Like Brianna's bolts?" I asked.

"Not as refined," she admitted. "It's still a bit random whether I hit my target, but I'm getting better."

"That could come in handy," I said.

"Did you learn anything more about your mother?" Brianna asked.

"Some," Sophie said. "I know she was killed by witches. I found the spot where she died and could see the signs of it still there after all this time."

"Powerful magic lingers," Brianna said, nodding.

"But what witches?" I asked.

"That part I'm still working on," she said. "Or I was until I hit a dead end. What I can tell you is I'm fairly certain it isn't related to Patricia and the others. I think a group that is active in the New Orleans area saw her and targeted her because she was a rogue witch on her own."

"A threat? Or just easy prey?" I asked.

Sophie shrugged. "Someone in New Orleans knows. Maybe lots of someones. But no one that was willing to talk to me."

"It makes sense that it wasn't related to Patricia's coven, though," Brianna said. "They locked themselves down in one place and time, far removed from where and when our mothers were. And we know my mother died of natural causes. She wasn't murdered for revenge."

"But what about my mother?" I asked.

"I don't know," Sophie said. "That sleet storm in August certainly sounds like magic. But it also sounds like she was just passing through when their car hit that tree. Maybe she was being pursued by witches, and that was just where they happened to catch up with her."

"But witches from where? Here?"

Sophie shrugged. "Maybe you have to go back to Iowa to find out for sure. Now that you know how to see magical things, that is."

"Maybe," I said. "But investigating something that happened two decades ago has to come second to saving Nick and Jackson."

"Maybe third," Brianna said, then took a deep breath. "That call I made was checking in with my team in Boston. They were doing the fact checking for me that I left undone to fly home. The last witch I saw told me something almost too crazy to be believed. But her story checks out. It *is* possible."

"Spill," Sophie said.

"This woman, Agnes Potter, claimed to be Miss Zenobia's closest friend," Brianna said. "So close that when she herself was in trouble, Miss Zenobia left the school to come to her aid."

"In 1968?" I guessed.

"Exactly. And she feels terribly guilty about that still. She didn't have any more details about that day than we knew already. That there was a fight, that the portal was nearly destroyed, and that our mothers—Miss Zenobia's dearest protégées—all disappeared."

"So what's the crazy rumor?" Sophie asked.

"That Miss Zenobia isn't dead," Brianna said.

"What?" Sophie and I gasped together.

"That's not possible, is it?" Sophie asked.

"I didn't think so," Brianna said. "But we found some texts in the hidden library that make me think that it just might be. It would require tremendous power, but Miss Zenobia would be one of the few witches in all of history who might be able to pull it off."

"How, though?" Sophie asked.

"Well, we know that she gave up years of her life to create a version of her self that could talk to us for a few minutes, right?" Brianna said. We both nodded. "This would be something similar. Actually, the spells are so related, I believe she must have done them at the same time."

"Which is why everyone thinks she died shortly after performing that other spell?" I asked.

"Yes, I think so."

"But if she isn't dead, where is she?" I asked.

"She put part of her self in that box for us to see," Sophie said slowly. "But where did the rest of her go?"

"In another box?" Brianna said, but she didn't sound sure.

"Wasn't there a body?" I asked. "What happened to it? Where are her remains?"

The three of us looked at each other, and I could tell we were all thinking the same thing.

The person who could answer all these questions was even now coming in through the back door with the last of Brianna and Sophie's luggage.

Mr. Trevor.

CHAPTER 11

$\mathcal{M}$r. Trevor smiled at all of us as we came into the kitchen.

"There you all are!" he said. "What are we thinking for supper? It's a bit late, but perhaps something light? I can heat up some leftover soup from the freezer. I think I even have a loaf of homemade bread in there still."

I bit my tongue before I could ask what sort of soup he was thinking of. We had to stay on topic.

"You have no idea how good that sounds," Sophie said, clasping her hands together in undisguised joy. "I've been eating far too much junk food since I was away."

"Auntie Claire didn't cook for you?" I asked.

"I paid her a visit when I first got there, but after a couple of days, I let her believe I had gone home again," Sophie said. "That was just to keep her safe in case what I was digging into turned out to be trouble. But, added bonus, I probably saved myself about ten pounds of weight gain. Auntie Claire cooks like everyone she's feeding is a hardworking farmhand in dire need of fuel."

"This isn't what we came down for," Brianna reminded us.

"No, you're right," Sophie said with regret. "Mr. Trevor, we needed to ask you a few questions."

Mr. Trevor's entire head was inside the freezer as he dug around until he found a storage container too frosted over for me to guess at its contents, and a perfectly divine-looking round loaf of bread inside a freezer bag.

"Questions?" he said. "Sounds serious."

"It is, rather," I said. "Maybe we should sit down."

"Certainly. Just give me a moment," he said. We watched as he put the soup into the microwave to defrost, then turned the dial on the toaster oven and put the bread inside. Only then did he join us at the kitchen table. "Fire away."

"We're wondering how well you remember the day Miss Zenobia died," I said.

Mr. Trevor's face fell, and I immediately regretted not finding a better way to phrase that question. I knew he had been fond of Miss Zenobia in a way that went a lot deeper than just her being his life-long employer.

"What did you want to know?" he asked. His voice was thick with grief, as if she had only died the day before. Sophie got up from the table and went to turn on the kettle for tea.

"Was someone with her when she died?" I asked.

"No," he said. "No, she died in her sleep."

"Who found her?" I asked. "You or Cynthia?"

"It was Cynthia," he said. "Cynthia said she was... already cold when she found her. She must have passed shortly after going to bed. Cynthia said it looked like she passed peacefully."

"The body was cold," Brianna said, and he nodded. "So Cynthia touched her?"

"What an odd question," Mr. Trevor said, but not in an offended way. He knew we were witches, and he knew witches often were compelled to ask odd questions. "I assume she must have."

"Did *you* touch the body?" I asked.

"No," he said and passed a hand over his face. "No, I couldn't bring myself to do that. You see, I had never touched her when she was alive. Not even once. I never even brushed up against her when I was bringing her tea. To touch her after she was dead? That would have been a violation. A blasphemy."

"She didn't want to be touched?" Sophie asked from where she was putting tea bags into mugs.

"I wouldn't say that," he said. He closed his eyes as if casting his mind back.

"Did you feel an aversion of some kind?" I asked, trying to phrase that as kindly as I could.

"No, not that either," he said, eyes still closed. "It was more like it wouldn't be proper. Or maybe even safe." His eyes opened, and he looked at each of us in turn. "Do you know the Greek myth about the woman who wanted to see Zeus in all his glory, and how even the smallest display of his power, when she saw it, was enough to burn her up?"

"Semele," Brianna murmured. Sophie and I exchanged a glance that confirmed we were both in the clueless club. But we got his point.

"To the best of my knowledge, no one ever touched her," Mr. Trevor said. "It wasn't a rule. No one ever told me not to or ever said anything about it. I just felt like it wasn't a thing I should do. Like if I did touch her, I would burn up, and nothing she could do would save me."

"So wait, Cynthia never touched her?" I asked.

Mr. Trevor sighed and pressed his fingertips to his temples. "I'm not being consistent, am I? And yet I remember both things."

"She told you the body was cold when she found it," Sophie said as she poured hot water into the mugs. "But she might not have said she knew that because she touched it."

"I think you're right," Mr. Trevor said.

"You didn't touch the body, but you did see it?" I asked.

"Only momentarily," Mr. Trevor said. "From her bedroom doorway. I didn't come any closer than that. I've seen other dead bodies before, my father and my grandparents. But I'd never seen a body that felt so diminished without its animating force. It was like Miss Zenobia, who had always been more alive than anyone, was also more dead. If that makes sense."

"It might," Brianna said. "Because it might not have actually been her body. She may have just left a shell behind that looked like her body. Did *no one* touch it?"

"A shell?" Mr. Trevor repeated, but didn't press his question. "I don't know what happened next, to be honest. Cynthia handled all the arrangements."

"What arrangements were made?" I asked.

"She was cremated," he said.

"Are the remains still here?" Brianna asked hopefully.

"No, they were sent back to her hometown in the United Kingdom," he said. "I don't think she had any living family left there, but there were other witches. I don't know the details. To be honest, I didn't want to know."

"Cynthia knew," I said. "But Cynthia is gone."

"Did Cynthia keep any sort of journal or paperwork? She must have had an office," Brianna said.

"There are official records, certainly," Mr. Trevor said. "Her law office was closed after she died, but all the files were moved to the office of a young lawyer she mentored through law school. I can have her pull them all out for you if you like. But I don't think they'll do much good. A big part of Cynthia's job was to provide an official version of things that were very different from what was actually going on, especially when it came to magical things."

"And this would have been a decidedly magical thing," Brianna sighed.

"Miss Tabitha in London would be a good place to start if you're looking for witches on that side of the pond," Mr. Trevor said. "I don't think she was Cynthia's contact for handling the remains, but she might know who was."

"We can look into that if we need to," Brianna said. "I think maybe we'll try a spell or two first."

Mr. Trevor took a sip of his tea, then, as if rejuvenated, got up from the table. "I'll need a few minutes yet to get this soup properly warmed up, and the bread as well."

"We'll be back down," I said. Then the three of us left the tantalizing aroma of warming bread behind to head back up to the library.

"I don't think she's in the UK," I said. "I think that was one of Cynthia's coverups."

"This is maddening," Sophie said. "The one person who could be the most help to us now is dead."

"No, none of that matters," Brianna said. "She wasn't cremated because she didn't die. What we're looking for is not remains, but her actual magical self."

"And that has to be here," I said, realizing Brianna was right. "That would be the whole point, right?"

"What's the whole point?" Sophie asked.

"She knew she was reaching the end of her unnatural lifespan," Brianna said. "The fight over the time portal nearly destroyed it. Miss Zenobia had invested a lot of her power—her self—into that portal. Her power would have been very much diminished, all in one blow, while her back was turned. She must have been very desperate in that moment."

"The last entry in the journal, she was about to go back into the portal to finish stabilizing it," Sophie said. "And to find her lost students, right?"

"And we don't know what happened next," Brianna said.

"We can form a theory, though," I said. "She did what she could with the portal, given that she was a very powerful witch but not one with time magic. Then she must have realized that all her students were out of her reach."

"But not right away," Sophie said. "She didn't, I guess, give up until just before we were summoned here. Right?"

"If she found us, she must have known that our mothers had jumped from 1968 to 1997," Brianna said. "She couldn't undo that."

"But did she find Patricia and the others?" I asked. "They were right there in the 1920s, just where she had fixed the time portal."

"Wait," Sophie said, holding up a hand as she struggled with her thoughts. "Our mothers aged. Time passed. After the fight, they landed in 1997 and time passed."

"No, after the fight, they were still in 1968," I said. "They were photographs in the newspaper. They didn't disappear through time until after."

"Oh, this is confusing," Sophie said, rubbing at her temples.

"And the others didn't appear in the 1920s either, at least not where Miss Zenobia could have found them," Brianna said. "They still look eighteen, right? So from 1968, they couldn't have landed much ahead of when we first met them. For all we know, they didn't appear until just before you and Otto first met Evanora."

"So if all her protégées were out of reach, she left the job of guarding the time bridge to us, and put herself in some sort of suspended animation?" I asked.

"First, she put just enough of her self into that box to give us the instructions we needed," Brianna said. "Then she created the shell of her body, maybe a physical structure or maybe just an illusion, but whatever it was that Mr. Trevor saw. Then she put the last of her self... wherever."

"Cynthia must have been in on it," I said. "She knew Miss Zenobia was not dead, but in magical suspended animation or whatever. No one moved the body, and nothing was cremated and sent away."

"Mr. Trevor *wasn't* in on the secret," Sophie said. "Okay. But why?"

"That's the real question, isn't it?" I said. "The part she put in the box was waiting for us to arrive and take up the calling. But what's the rest of her waiting for?"

"Let's at least try a spell to find her," Brianna said.

We settled together on the open expanse of carpet under the front windows, cross-legged in a circle with our knees nearly touching. We fell into a trance state where our energy flowed from one to the other, and we were all conscious of each other.

It was like we had never been apart; like we'd still been doing this every day. And I, who had never left, had the strangest feeling of coming home.

I sensed the exhaustion headache resting behind Brianna's eyes, the pain Sophie was hiding from us because she hadn't learned more about her mother's fate.

I wondered what they were sensing from me.

Then Brianna guided our collective attention to our memory of Miss Zenobia from the night of the reading of her will, when we had seen her ghostly form and promised to carry on her duty to guard this place. Together, our focus was so intense I could almost see her floating before us with her severe, steel gray hair and fearsome eyes.

We expanded our awareness, trying to sense where she might be hiding. The house was filled with a sense of her, like magical fingerprints all over everything. But it wasn't her. We searched the house from top to bottom, but there was nothing.

Brianna was about to release us out of the trance when I felt Sophie pulling us into the backyard, to where the remains of the portal touched our time. We weren't seeing through my eyes, and without that perception of the world as threads, the portal was all but invisible.

Then Mr. Trevor called up the stairs that dinner was ready, and we all opened our eyes at once.

And both Brianna and Sophie were looking at me.

"What have you been up to?" Sophie asked.

"What do you mean?" I asked, but I could feel my cheeks flushing dark red.

"You have a glow," Brianna said.

"You've been doing more than working with your wand," Sophie said.

"Obviously I can't do that twenty-four hours a day," I said.

"I'm not accusing you of not practicing enough," Sophie said with raised brows.

"You glow," Brianna said again, and I finally realized she wasn't talking about some visual clue of my active love life.

"Your power is off the charts," Sophie said. "But your control as well. You didn't even come close to burning us with it, but what you were flowing into us was..."

"Amazing," Brianna finished. But she didn't sound impressed. She sounded scared.

"What have you been doing?" Sophie asked again.

I wanted so badly not to answer. I wanted to find something flippant to say, something with just enough truth in it to satisfy them so we could all go downstairs and eat together like old times.

But this time when I opened my mouth, the truth came out. "I've been feeling different since we collapsed the portal," I said.

"Different how?" Sophie asked.

"Invincible," I said, then quickly added, "-ish."

"Inviciblish," Sophie repeated.

"I don't think that's a word?" Brianna said.

"I feel stronger. Like I can do anything," I said. "Which doesn't mean I've been taking chances. I'm very, very careful."

"You're very, very careful while you do what exactly?" Sophie asked.

I could feel both of their eyes on me, pinning me down. I fought the urge to squirm. "I've been going back to 1928 without you two."

"But we collapsed the portal," Brianna said.

"I know," I said. "I've been checking it daily. No one else is using it. But I can. I can sort of reduce my form to a stream of particles and pass through it, then reassemble on the other side. At least, that's what it feels like is happening."

"I *have* to observe this," Brianna said, whipping out her notebook to start scribbling notes in it. Sophie shot her an annoyed look that she missed completely.

"How many times have you done this little trick?" Sophie asked.

"Daily," I said. "Or almost."

"There and back again," Sophie said. "Oh, you really mean twice daily?"

My cheeks flushed even hotter, and I worried I was about to burst blood vessels.

"Oh. I see," Sophie said. "Daily it is."

"I've been working with Otto and Edward to find the coven," I said. "It looked like they were either deep underground or gone from the city entirely. Or at least I thought so until this thing with Jackson and Nick came up."

"So, what do we do now?" Brianna asked, pen still poised over the page, as if prepared to write down whatever was said next.

Sophie sighed. "Now we eat," she said. "I'm starving. But that's not why I'm grumpy," she added, pointing a finger at me.

I raised my hands in surrender.

"But then what?" Brianna asked.

"What choice do we have?" Sophie said. "There's nothing we can do here. We have to go back to 1928."

Brianna put her notebook away, her hair not quite hiding the wide grin on her face. Sophie might be grumpy, but Brianna was geeked out of her mind.

She wasn't just going to observe moving through a wormhole. She was going to get to experience it firsthand.

"I'm so glad you guys are home," I said. Sophie rolled her eyes, but I could tell she felt the same way.

CHAPTER 12

$\mathcal{B}$efore we had even finished eating, my phone dinged to let me know that Nick's grandfather's sister had written a very lengthy response to my email. I finished off my bowl of soup and brought a hunk of bread with me up to my computer in the library, where I could more easily read what she had written to me.

I admit it was a bit alarming, as she spun her tale, just how many people she had contacted to verify parts of the story. All of Chippewa Falls must be really wondering who I was and why I cared.

But she had really come through. She had tracked down two women whose age was nearly into triple digits but who remembered the story well, told to them by older siblings back in the day. It was clear that though Mr. Schmidt had lived all his days alone in what had once been his parents' house, he was less a surly hermit and more a genuinely shy man who never recovered from one horrifically embarrassing night. Everyone spoke of him in fondness, and with genuine regret for how things turned out.

The logical part of me found it interesting, how everyone seemed to really feel that things had been meant to turn out some other way. Like they all could sense on some small level that something had been altered from the natural flow.

But the bigger, more emotional part of me felt more guilt than ever. Nick was gone, Jackson was gone, unnamed and unnumbered relatives of Nick were also gone. And this man's life, although it had carried on for its requisite years, had been destroyed all the same.

All just to get to me.

I pushed my feelings aside and scanned the email again for the information I needed.

The story went that poor Mr. Robert Schmidt had pined for the same girl from afar all through high school. Then, at the spring dance, he had been all prepared to make his move, when some strange girl no one knew—some other fellow's date was the general assumption—had dumped several glasses of red punch all over him.

So one of Patricia's witches, under the cloak and hood, was young enough to pass as a high school student's date.

But that didn't matter. What mattered was the name of the girl he was supposed to dance with that night. Dance with and marry and raise many children with.

And there it was. Dorothy Schreiber.

I went back downstairs to where Brianna and Sophie were waiting for me in the solarium. They were dressed for a cold April evening in 1928.

"I don't suppose you need anything from us at all," Sophie said. Eating dinner had only taken the barest edge off her bad mood.

"On the contrary, I think it would be a very good idea for us to pool our energy," I said. "As I told you, I've been very, very careful. I check everything on this end before going through the wormhole, then check everything on that end before I make a move."

"Your growing power must be attracting the coven's attention," Brianna said.

"It might have done, if I wasn't using your cloak every time I travel," I said, pointing to the warded cloak still hanging on a hook by the back door.

"You should wear it again," Brianna said. "And you have Cynthia's amulet?"

"I never take it off," I said, pulling down the collar of my shirt so they could see it there.

"We have ours as well," Sophie said, and Brianna nodded.

"Then we're all set," I said, hoping my briskness didn't sound too forced.

We went out to the orchard and sat in a circle on the ground. Again, our energy flowed through us with effortless ease. I could sense the world as Sophie did and found no trace of danger. I could see it all as a series of causes and effects all interconnected like an elaborate clockwork, much as Brianna did. Everything was just as it should be.

I could feel the other two agreeing with my assessment, then directing their energies towards me. Now it was my turn.

I shifted into the world of threads and saw at once that Sophie had grown in power, just as she had told us, but so had Brianna. They looked bright enough that, combined with my own power, I didn't think we had much to fear from Patricia and her coven, even though they outnumbered us by quite a bit.

I puzzled for a moment about the best way to move us all through the wormhole and decided I should start with one of the other two, then go second myself, and bring the last along behind me. Whoever went first might be a bit vulnerable, but being in the middle, I'd be aware of both ends at once. It was the safest bet.

I started with Sophie. I felt a spike of panic race through her, but this was quickly dissipated by her own force of will. She settled into a meditative calm even as I broke her form into a stream of particles and channeled them through the portal, which was so tight she hadn't even sensed it with her own powers.

Her calm and trust washed over me, but at the same time, I felt all of Brianna's excitement as she processed what was happening.

I felt Sophie reforming on the other side, standing in the colder, snowier weather of 1928. Then I followed behind her. There was a brief moment where I wasn't quite aware of either of them, not emotionally and especially not physically. But it was only a blink in time, and then I was growing in awareness in the younger orchard beside Sophie.

At last, I pulled Brianna through behind me, and she reformed beside us with an immense grin on her face.

"I have to do that again," she said.

"Of course you do," Sophie said. "How else are we going to get home?"

"You know what I meant," Brianna said. "So, what's the plan now?"

"We go to Edward's apartment," I said, and started to lead the way down the garden path.

"Wouldn't here be safer?" Sophie asked as she fell into step beside me.

"Maybe for us, but not for them," I said. "I've put wards all around Edward's building and on the street. Actually, I'd like Brianna to see it anyway, to see if there's anything I should add to keep him safe."

"That's where you've been? When you come back to 1928?" Brianna asked.

"Otto meets us there," I said.

"So just there every time," Sophie said. "You haven't gone looking for the witches."

"I *did* have Otto drive me around their block so I could see if they had anything to do with the missing boy," I admitted. "But we didn't stop the car. And I was careful. Anyway, they didn't seem to be around."

Sophie didn't answer, but I could feel disapproval radiating off of her.

It was nearly ten at night, but I could tell that Edward was both home and awake from the light beaming out from his bare, if filthy, window. I led the way up the steps and knocked once before letting myself in.

He must have been standing right at the door, perhaps drawn there by the sound of the three of us coming up the stairs, because before I had taken more than a step into the apartment, I was in his arms.

"You're late," he said, squeezing me tightly. "You're late."

"Am I?" I asked, looking over his shoulder at Otto standing by the table.

"I don't know what your arrangements were," he said with a shrug. "I just know he's been in a state since sundown."

"I'm sorry, Edward. I didn't mean to worry you," I said. "Brianna and Sophie came back today. I guess in all the activity, I forgot what we said last time."

Sophie came in the door, giving Otto a careless wave. Brianna trailed behind, eyes faraway as she scanned the apartment. She wasn't assessing furniture; I could tell she was checking out all the wards.

"Very good," she said, her voice as distant as her eyes. "Very thorough."

"Thanks," I said, giving Edward a little smile. "I was motivated to make this a very safe space."

"I have boys outside as well," Otto said.

"I didn't see any," Sophie said.

"If you could see them, they wouldn't be any good at their jobs. And I put my best boys on Edward."

"The boys I knew about," Edward said. "What have you been up to, then?"

"Just some magic stuff," I said. "And it was as much about keeping me safe when I'm here as it was keeping you safe when I'm not."

"I still feel rather smothered," he said.

"With love?"

He laughed, and I gave him a kiss, ignoring Sophie rolling her eyes at me.

"I do have some tidbits about the witches," Otto said. "If you'd gotten here any later, I'd have missed getting it to you."

"What do you have?" I asked.

"Nothing about that boy you were looking for," he said. "I'm not sure how I can help with that. No, this is about that earlier thing. Seeing if they've ranged outside of St. Paul. They have."

"Let me guess," I said. "Chippewa Falls?"

Otto gaped, then sat down on the arm of the couch as if he were about to fall down. "Yes, as a matter of fact."

"All of them, or just a few?" I asked.

One for sure," he said. "I've sent more boys that way to get more details."

"I can imagine what that investigation must be like," Sophie said under her breath.

"I don't know if there's anything more to learn there," I said. "I know what that witch was up to, and she's already done it. She's probably back in St. Paul by now."

"What was she up to?" Otto asked.

I moved over to hunch over the table to write two names on a scrap of paper. "There is a young man living there named Robert Schmidt. He was meant to meet the love of his life at a dance last weekend. Her name is Dorothy Schreiber. They were supposed to dance together, fall in love, marry and have a son. Probably more kids. Plus grandkids. And Great-grandkids. Among whom is a certain police officer who's been helping us in 2019."

"You work with the police?" Otto asked. I'm not sure his air of offense was entirely feigned.

"In training," I said. "But yes. He's important to... us. And they've managed to wipe him out of existence just by making sure this couple in Chippewa Falls never meets." I pushed the paper towards him, and he picked it up.

"They've wiped out all those people?" Edward asked. "Generations of people? Just like that?"

"I thought you were trying to find a boy?" Otto asked.

"Him too," I said. "He's not related, and his name is so common, I doubt I'll ever find out who his ancestors were." I felt my cheeks heating but tried to fight it down by force of will. Hopefully, coming in from the cold would explain it. But I could feel Otto looking at me and knew he knew I was lying through my teeth. "But I'm sure they got rid of him the same way," I went on. "I have no idea why, though. He had no connection to me."

"Maybe he was practice," Otto said.

"That's an evil thought," Sophie said.

"If you need to get to Chippewa Falls, my car is at your disposal," he said.

"No, there's nothing we three can do there," I said. "We can't go back in time to stop whatever witch was behind this from interfering with the proper flow of time. I don't think we can fix it."

"So your police officer friend is just gone forever?" Edward asked.

I couldn't answer around the lump in my throat. There had to be something we could do. Nick couldn't just be gone.

Edward held me close as I fought back the tears. Otto leaned closer to Sophie. "Who is this guy?"

"I don't know," Sophie said. "Brianna and I don't remember him. Only Amanda does."

I felt Edward stiffen a bit, but if he was entertaining jealous thoughts, he chose not to speak them out loud.

"He's a friend," I said. "I don't have a lot of those. Pretty much all my other friends are in this room."

"So what's the plan, then?" Otto asked.

"You have boys there already, right?" I asked.

He nodded. "Four, as it happens. Watching every move your witch makes."

"Good," I said. The sudden feeling of relief was a rush to my head. Finally, something was going our way. "That's perfect. Make sure they stay in contact; we might end up needing them. But they're definitely Plan B."

"And what's Plan A?" Otto asked. But I could tell it was a rhetorical question. He knew exactly what I was thinking.

"There's only ever really been one plan A, hasn't there?" I said. "A plan I've put off implementing for far too long."

"What plan?" Edward asked. But I could tell by the fear in his voice he too already knew what I was going to say. I caught his hand and gave it a reassuring squeeze before turning back to the others.

"We take the fight to them."

CHAPTER 13

Otto circled the block several times until Brianna and Sophie agreed that all was as quiet as I had said it was.

"That doesn't mean it's safe," Sophie said. She was sitting in the front seat next to Otto, eyes still sweeping over everything even as she spoke. "It just means the trouble is waiting for us inside."

"Which is fine," I said. "We knew we came here for a fight."

"Can't we try talking first?" Brianna asked. She leaned forward to look at me from around Edward, who was wedged in between us in the back seat. "They erased your friend, and I know that makes you mad. But even you said they did it to get your attention. If it was a fight they were after, they could have just ambushed us when we emerged from the portal."

"If they just wanted my attention, they could have left a message at the school, or literally a million other things," I said. "They didn't have to hurt our friend."

"Amanda," Edward said, touching my arm to be sure he had my attention. "Maybe Brianna is right. Maybe they aren't just looking for a fight."

"I'm not going in unprepared," I said, clutching my wand.

"I'm not saying that," he said. "I'm saying, be prepared for a fight, yes, but also be prepared for a negotiation."

"If Patricia wants anything, it's the same thing she wanted before," I said. "For me to help her perform time magic. And last time, that was a trap."

"So we'll be prepared for that too," Sophie said. She sort of tossed the words back over her shoulder, her eyes still scanning everything around us. "Look, our magic is hiding us, but I don't think it will work forever. Not with us just circling their perimeter. If we're going in, let's do it now."

"Agreed," I said, leaning over the back of the front seat to point past Otto's shoulder. "Pull over there."

"There's no place to park," he said.

"You're not going to park," I said. "You and Edward are dropping us off and getting back to his place. You'll be safe there."

"Safe for how long?" Otto asked.

"Those wards will outlive me, if that's what you're asking," I said. "But if we don't come out of this, they have no reason to target you, anyway."

Otto made a gesture somewhere between a shrug and a nod, then wove his way through traffic to pull up to the curb at the end of a driveway.

"You're coming out of this," Edward said.

"Of course I am," I said. "Otto just likes to cover all the angles. You know that."

"You're coming out of this," he said again, pressing his forehead to mine.

"I'll be back before you know it," I said. Our kiss was ruined by Otto's aggressive braking. Sophie and Brianna jumped out of their doors, Brianna scurrying around the car as Sophie wrenched my door open, pulling me out of the car and ruining my second attempt at a kiss goodbye.

"Be safe," Otto said, looking like he'd kill us if we didn't.

It was clearly all Edward could do to keep himself in the car and not go charging after us. I wanted to tell him again that I would be safe, and we'd be back together in no time, but Otto pulled away before I could get the words out. The car rocketed back into traffic, and I lost sight of it even before I could raise my hand to wave goodbye.

"Come on," Sophie said, gripping her wand despite the three of us being in very public view. "This alley is heading in the right direction."

"Everything looks different," I said as we picked our way over sunken cobblestones and around stagnant pools of what I really hoped was just water. "How much of this is glamour?"

"The warehouse we went to before was never real," Sophie said. "It looked real to me at the time, though. And everything looks real to me now." She was chewing her lip fiercely enough I was worried she'd draw blood.

"Our skills have grown since the last time we were here," Brianna said. "But maybe theirs did too."

"That's a scary thought," I said.

"I think it's a point to put in the 'negotiate first' column," Brianna said.

The alley ended at a narrower cross-alley that ran perpendicular to the one we were standing in. We paused at the intersection to look both ways.

Both ended in shadowy darkness. Brianna spoke a few arcane words, and two balls of light erupted from the end of her wand. They took off in opposite directions, one following the alley to our left, the other to our right.

They were both quickly swallowed up by the darkness after only a few yards of gliding over wetter and wetter cobblestones.

"Which way then?" Sophie asked.

"As much as I hate the idea of sitting down in this... whatever it is, I think we need to circle up and work together," I said.

Sophie frowned, sharing my aversion, but Brianna just nodded and plopped cross-legged down on the ground. Sophie and I joined her.

Our combined consciousness quickly decided there was no point in using our sensing abilities separately. We'd each been using our own since Otto had started circling the block, to no avail. Instead, we combined our senses into one, something we had never done before.

I felt the other two sort of gasp and realized that this newfound drive to synthesize new abilities was coming from me. And it scared them more than a little. But at the moment, we really needed it.

And it worked. Looking through three pairs of magical eyes at once, we were finally able to see that the tower still stood. Eldritch light danced up its sides, illuminating the sky overhead as it reflected greenly off the clouds. It looked taller than I remembered it, but it also felt changed in other ways. The art déco features were starting to morph into something with a lot less optimism.

It hadn't been built as a testament to industry and the ambitions of the wealthy. It hadn't been built at all. It simply existed to tower over everything. The fact that nearly no one in its shadow could even see it wasn't even a problem. I suspected, in ways none of them could define, everyone in St. Paul felt it. It was oppressive.

I really wanted to tear it down.

We all opened our eyes at the same moment.

"Neither alley," Sophie said, getting up and making a sweeping gesture with her wand to clean the back of her skirt.

"Right," Brianna agreed. "Straight through that wall."

"Which isn't a wall," I said. "Are we ready?"

We all held up our wands, then advanced on the wall.

I was rather hoping the illusion would drop before we got there, but if the witches were even aware we were at their front door, they weren't going to so blatantly invite us in. We had to keep walking, straight through the cold stone.

And it was really cold, and not just physically. It was like having an entire army of devils dancing on your grave.

But it only lasted a moment. Then we were stepping into the tower's interior. For a second, I thought we were alone. Perhaps the members of the coven were still in Wisconsin or scattered in all directions.

But before we were quite in the center of the room, they began to appear around us, stepping out of the marble pillars.

That was unnerving. They hadn't been hiding behind them. They had been hiding *in* them.

I held my wand out, ready to bathe anyone in fire who looked like they were about to do something aggressive. Brianna and Sophie stepped out of my line of sight as the three of us formed a different sort of circle: on our feet, shoulders touching, prepared to fight back to back. I could already hear Brianna murmuring words under her breath.

"We aren't looking for a fight." I recognized the voice as Patricia's, but with the way the walls of the tower's open interior echoed, I couldn't tell which of the cloaked and hooded figures it was coming from.

"Aren't you?" I asked, pointing my wand at one figure and then the next as I hunted for her. "You killed my friend."

"Killed?" she said. "No, not killed."

"He's gone," I said. "You erased his very birth."

"Nothing has been done that can't be undone," she said. "We were very careful about that."

A figure just at the corner of my eye started walking forward, and I spun to aim my wand that way. The figure lifted her hands to show they were empty, then raised them to throw back her hood.

It was Patricia.

She didn't look good. She looked like she'd been fighting some sort of wasting disease, fighting it for years. Fighting it some place far from sunlight. Her skin was more grayish than pale, her hair was thinning to near baldness, and her eyes were sinking into her skull.

But the light in those eyes was undiminished.

"Is this a glamour?" I demanded.

"I'm afraid not," she said, and as she continued to walk closer to the three of us, I detected a limp she was striving hard to hide.

Or faking really well.

"You did this to me," she said. "You've cut me off from my power. I'm dying. I need your help."

"You could've left word through the school," I said. "You didn't need to kill my friend."

"A message wouldn't be enough, I was afraid," she said. She was nearly within an arm's reach, but when I gestured with my wand, she came to a halt, once more lifting her hands to show she held no wand. "I needed leverage."

"Leverage? You've destroyed how many lives?"

It was a rhetorical question, and she knew it, but even sick as she appeared to be, that light in her eyes still wanted to gloat. "Let's see; we undid four children, twelve grandchildren, and twenty great-grandchildren. I guess that makes thirty-six?" She looked to one of the other figures, who nodded to confirm her math.

"Don't forget Jackson," I said. "That makes thirty-seven."

A momentary confusion passed over her eyes, but was quickly gone. She went on as if I hadn't spoken at all. "But it served its purpose. I've destroyed the one thing you loved best in this world. Your one true love, yes? But I can put him back. I can bring them all back. All you have to do is help me fix what you did to the time portal."

I've never played poker, and I don't generally have a need to lie to people or hide my feelings. But at that moment, I desperately needed to have a poker face.

She had gone after Nick because she thought he was my one true love? How had she gotten such a skewed idea of our relationship?

I wished I had felt some sort of triumph that I had fooled her somehow, but all I felt was guilt. Nick had been eliminated, over a misunderstanding, because of me. I think my guilt was all the greater for the fact that he wasn't even the one I loved.

But greater than my guilt was my fear. What if Patricia discovered she was wrong about Nick? What if she found out about Edward? Edward, who was practically in her reach? Pretty much all she could have done to Nick was what she did. What more was she capable of, with Edward physically in her clutches?

Tears pricked at the corners of my eyes, and my face wanted to collapse with sorrow. I couldn't do it. I couldn't hide what I was feeling.

But then Sophie's hand brushed my arm and an eerie calm washed over the surface of my mind. All of those feelings were still there, but deeper.

I couldn't see myself, but I was certain my face had the quietly superior look that Sophie always wore. I had long suspected she used it to protect herself from others knowing what she was thinking and feeling. It felt weird being on the other side of that.

Patricia's eyes were narrowed, though. I might have summoned that mask too late. She had gotten a glimpse of my feelings. But she hadn't known what I was thinking. She still didn't know about Edward.

I had to keep it that way.

"How did you know about Nick?" I asked. "You've never even met him."

"We were aware of everything happening in the vicinity of that wardrobe," she said.

"Liar," I said. "You didn't even know I existed until I met Evanora."

"Not quite true," Patricia said, holding up a finger like a professor clarifying a point in a lecture. "I was aware of you, your power, your magical presence. But you are correct, until Evanora laid eyes on you, we didn't know who you were in the mundane sense. We got up to speed on you and every facet of your life before we returned the wardrobe to you." She leaned to one side to look past me to Brianna. "Very lovely warding, by the way. Of course, we were quite done with it before we let it go, so it was not really necessary, but top marks for effort."

"How did the wardrobe lead you to Nick?" I asked.

"Your skills are not as refined as mine, you know," she said, turning her attention back to me. "I can see the entire history of an object, any moment in its time."

"He was with me the first time I saw it," I remembered.

Patricia gave a nod. "I could see the blooming connection between you. The beginning of a lifelong story."

"Apparently an ill-fated one," I said, gripping my wand still more tightly.

"Not necessarily," Patricia said. "I can undo what I did. As I said, this wasn't an attack. It was just leverage. I need to know that when we delve into time magic together, you won't take the opportunity to completely destroy me."

"And what leverage do I have?" I demanded.

The shock on her face certainly looked genuine. Her eyes darted to Brianna, then to Sophie, and then back to me. "What leverage do you need? You're the one with all the power."

CHAPTER 14

That might have been the last thing I expected her to say. I certainly didn't know how to respond to it.

"I need a moment to confer with my friends," I said.

"Of course," Patricia said, taking several steps back.

I turned to face Sophie and Brianna. Brianna raised her wand and spoke a few words. At first, I thought she was doing the umbrella spell despite the fact we were more or less indoors. But as the edges of the umbrella over us extended down to the floor, all the echoing sounds of a dozen witches in swishing robes were cut off.

"Can they hear us?" I asked.

"We should probably assume they can," Brianna said.

So no talk of Edward, but I could see in their eyes that Sophie and Brianna were also thinking of him. They would do as much to protect him as I would. That was a comfort.

"So..." I said leadingly.

"It's a trap, obviously," Sophie said. "She's not even trying to pretend it isn't."

"What about how sick she looks?" I asked. "Is that a glamour?"

"Who knows?" Brianna said. "Even if it's real, it might not have anything to do with us."

"If it's because of the fight to protect the time portal, I feel no guilt for that," Sophie said.

"Nor I," I said. "She's not going to make me feel bad when she's the one who started that fight."

"No, the real question is, do we need her to save Nick?" Sophie asked.

"We could go to Wisconsin ourselves," Brianna said. "We could figure out a way to get that couple back together without Patricia."

"Or have Otto's boys do it," Sophie said. "Although how they'd pull it off might be interesting to see."

"She'll be expecting us to try that, though, won't she?" I asked.

"You're right," Brianna said with a sigh. "We try to get them together; she breaks them up again. That much mucking with the timeline..." She shook her head.

"I don't think there will be that many moves and countermoves," Sophie said. "If we try anything, she'll just kill one of them. Game, set and match."

"And there's still Jackson," I said. "She didn't seem to know Jackson. Was he an accident? Or does she just not care?"

"She was confused for a second, but she dropped it pretty quick," Sophie said. "I'd file that under 'doesn't care.' But it's the same as with Nick. If we try to fix things ourselves, she will countermove to the extreme."

"So it's a fight, then?" Brianna asked.

"I thought you didn't want a fight," I said.

"I didn't. I still don't. But if they are mucking with timelines, we have to do something. We have a duty," she said.

"Can we win a fight?" Sophie asked.

I was wondering the same thing myself. A part of me really wanted to know the answer to that, was willing to do anything to find out.

That part of me was starting to scare the rest of me.

"Negotiation," I said. "That's what we said we wanted to start with."

"Patricia has leverage," Sophie said. "We don't."

"Unless she's right about my power," I said.

"Is she?" Brianna asked. "Do you feel that much stronger?"

"I don't know," I said. "But there is a symmetry there that makes a kind of sense. I'm stronger, and she's weaker."

"I don't want to make any decisions based on the idea that she's as weak as she looks," Sophie said. "Not when we can't tell lie from truth."

"We can," I said. "If we all look together."

We sat down on the floor and flowed our energy into one another, then turned our attention to Patricia.

It only took a glance. We blinked back into the world, still under the cover of Brianna's silencing spell.

"How is she even standing?" Sophie wondered.

"So we agree it's real," I said. "It's also really weird. It's not any kind of injury or sickness I've ever seen."

"She says she'll die without your help. I guess I believe her," Brianna said.

"So we're negotiating with a desperate woman who holds dozens of lives in her hands," Sophie said. "I don't like it."

"Do we have another choice?" I asked. "Either I do as she asks, or we fight them all."

"I don't like either option," Sophie said.

"But is she as weakened in the world of threads as she is here?" Brianna wondered. "It would be just you and her there. Sophie and I couldn't help you, but these other witches couldn't help her, either. Is that a good thing or a bad thing?"

We lapsed into silence for several moments, then Sophie straightened.

"What is it?" I asked.

"She's trying to get our attention," Sophie said. "There's nothing more for us to discuss here. We might as well see what she wants."

I looked to Brianna, who nodded. She dropped her spell, and we all three turned to Patricia.

"I understand why you are reluctant to trust me," Patricia said. "I've spoken with the others, and we'd like to make a gesture. A gift to demonstrate our goodwill."

"What sort of gift?" I asked.

Patricia just smiled. Then she gestured to two of the other witches, who threw back their hoods as they approached. It was her two classmates from the last class of Miss Zenobia Weekes' Charm School for Exceptional Young Ladies.

"We see that the three of you have been learning how working together enhances your power," she said as the others came to stand beside her. "The specific focus of each power interlocks with other powers to create something new. Yes?"

"Get to the point," I said, not willing to discuss what the three of us were capable of. Not with the enemy.

"My magic is time and story, as you know. Debra doesn't just erase or fabricate memories; she can also enhance them. And Linda's glamour makes anything she can imagine into something everyone can see," she said.

"I thought your power was weakened at the moment," I said.

"It is," she said. "But my part in this is small enough that I'll manage. We won't be moving through time or manipulating it in any way."

"What *will* you be doing?" Sophie asked.

Patricia unclasped her robe and let it fall to the ground at her feet, then unbuttoned the top of her sweater to tug at something around her neck. I expected an amulet of some sort, and I sensed Brianna and Sophie on either side of me stiffening as if expecting an attack. But it was just a necklace, a simple piece of turquoise on a braided loop of leather. It didn't look particularly magical.

It just looked like something a hippie would wear. And as much as Patricia had been a teenager in the sixties, I was pretty sure she was the farthest thing from a hippie.

"What is that?" I asked.

"Just a necklace," she said, slipping it off from around her neck then holding it out for us to see. "Check it for enchantments if you like. It has no magical properties."

I didn't want to go to the world of threads, not while standing so close to Patricia. I looked over at Brianna, then at Sophie, and they both gave me a nod.

"All right," I said. "If it's not magical, what is it?"

"Just something I was wearing that day," she said. "The day the three of us were thrown here. The day we fought your mothers. Of course, Debra and Linda could just use their powers to show you our own memories of the day, but I have a feeling you'd think we were biased or even lying to you."

"You think?" Sophie mumbled under her breath.

Patricia ignored her. "With my magic, I can tell part of the story of this necklace. All the things it witnessed on that day."

"And how do we know that won't be a lie?" I asked.

Patricia blinked as if surprised by the question. "Just do what you did a moment ago. When you look through each other's eyes all at once, you'll see if we're deceiving you."

"What do you get out of this?" I asked.

"Goodwill," she said. "You'll see that we don't want to fight you. Everything between you and us has been a series of misunderstandings. We've been talking about it amongst ourselves since the last time we encountered you, and we've agreed that you three aren't the bad guys."

"Gee, thanks," I said.

"You thought we were bad guys?" Brianna asked. She sounded a little hurt.

"And you thought the same of us, didn't you?" Patricia said.

"You attacked us," Sophie said.

"Because we didn't understand who and what you really were," she said. "We just want to give you the same opportunity to see that about us."

"You're not acting like good guys," I said. "Taking a hostage for leverage might be a gray area, but destroying so many lives to take one, just one, as leverage? There's no gray in that at all."

"Nothing has been done that can't be undone," Patricia said. "You know how time works as well as I, surely. You know I speak the truth. No one is really gone yet. Not irretrievably."

"Just see," Debra said. "See what the amulet has to show you. Talk about it amongst yourselves. Then decide."

I looked at Sophie, then at Brianna.

"We probably should," Brianna said.

"I agree," Sophie said. "But I'm keeping my skepticism meter cranked all the way up."

"I would expect no less," Patricia said. "Shall we?"

CHAPTER 15

The six of us formed a circle, but not evenly spaced. The three of them clustered on one side, Patricia in the center, with Linda on her right and Debra on her left.

We did the same on our side, with Brianna in the middle and Sophie on her right and me on her left. Patricia raised an eyebrow at this, but whatever she thought about the current level of power I had, Brianna was always the one we put in charge when the three of us worked together. She had studied more about magic than Sophie or I was ever going to know. Raw power couldn't compare with that kind of grounding in the fundamentals.

Debra and Linda had also taken off their long robes before sitting down beside Patricia. They were still dressed like three young women who wished it were still the sixties, but not as extravagantly as the last time we had seen them. The first time we'd seen them, they'd been dressed for the fashion runway. Now it was bell-bottomed jeans and peasant tops, and Patricia's wasn't the only piece of turquoise jewelry.

Patricia put that necklace in the center of the circle. "I don't need to touch it to tell its story," she said. "And this way, you know I'm not hiding anything from you."

She took Debra's hand in her left and Linda's in her right, then took a deep breath, eyes half-closed as she gazed at the necklace on the marble floor. Debra kept a light grasp on Patricia's hand but reached her other hand to touch just a fingertip to Patricia's temple. Now her eyes were half-closed, her gaze directed towards the floor but not fixed on anything, and Patricia's eyes closed.

Brianna pulled Sophie and me into her awareness, and we were looking through all our eyes at once again. I was still hesitant to truly see with my own brand of magic. The last time I had gone into the world of threads here had not gone well. But even without that vision, the three of us could feel the power building on the far side of the circle.

Then Debra took her hand away from Patricia's forehead, reaching across her towards Linda. Linda stretched her free hand across her own body and Patricia's to touch her fingertips to Debra's. Debra closed her eyes as Linda's gaze went unfixed. Then finally she closed her eyes as well.

For a moment, nothing happened. We could feel the power they were flowing through themselves building in intensity, but we had no idea what they were preparing to do with it.

Then Patricia opened her eyes with a loud gasp of breath, much as I did myself when I spent too long out of my body. The other two remained in motionless meditative silence.

Then Patricia looked back down at the necklace in between us. It flashed as if her eyes were casting beams of light on it. Then the flash became a cone of brightness. Then forms began to appear inside that cone. The forms gained definition until I realized we were inside one of the bedrooms at the charm school. Someone was sitting up in the bed and looking around the room.

It wasn't like watching a movie. It was more like watching someone play a first-person shooter game. But the POV wasn't the person in the bed, presumably Patricia. It was the necklace she was wearing.

The view swooped dizzily for a moment as this unseen version of Patricia swung her legs out of bed, then crept down the staircase.

That was when I realized we weren't just seeing what had

happened. There was audio too. As she avoided every squeak on the steps—squeaks I knew all too well from my own midnight treks for snacks—I figured out why she was sneaking around. There were voices whispering together in the foyer.

She stopped the moment the tops of three heads came into view. I couldn't see their faces, but I knew the hair from photographs. My mother with her hair a lighter blonde than mine, finer too and perfectly straight. Sophie's mother's hair styled in a glistening afro. Brianna's mother's hair was more red than gold and curlier than Brianna's, but recognizable all the same.

"You're sure she's gone?" Sophie's mother Marie said. I had never heard her speak before, but that bossy tone I knew intimately from her daughter.

"We saw her leave," my mother Kathleen said.

"They called me from Boston the moment she arrived," Brianna's mother Lula said. To my surprise, she had a thick Boston accent, whereas Brianna, who had also grown up there, had none. "She's already deep in spellwork with the other witch. We'll never have a better chance than we do now."

"We've waited so long already. It has to be today," my mother said.

"Are you sure you're up to this?" Marie asked. My mother's head bent a little, and I could imagine her stroking what was a very pregnant belly.

"I've been training," my mother said. "I know the baby makes my energy unstable, but I can handle it. We have to do this."

"We'll have to be fast," Marie said. "If she senses what we're up to, she'll be on us in the blink of an eye."

"The spellwork she's doing in Boston is very intensive," Lula said. "She's not even entirely in this realm at the moment."

"Extremely distracted," my mother said. "We couldn't ask for a more perfect moment."

"I could ask for a baby not to be involved," Marie said, "but all right. This is the time. Wands at the ready?"

Three wand tips appeared beside their heads with military precision.

"Let's do this," Lula said.

They all sounded so grim. Three soldiers about to undertake some impossible task that simply had to be done but was not likely to be a success.

Why?

I saw them move out of the foyer, down the corridor towards the back of the house. But Patricia didn't follow them. Instead, she ran back up the stairs. Even in her haste, she was silent, and I suspected she did a lot of eavesdropping on the stairs.

Then she burst into the library where Linda and Debra were laughing together over something in the magazine spread out between them.

"They're here!" she said in a furious whisper. "I told you! I told you they'd do it! Why didn't Miss Zenobia believe me?"

"We have to call her," Debra said, running to a phone on the library wall that no longer existed in my own time.

"Too late!" Patricia hissed, putting her hand over Debra's to keep her from picking up the handset. "Lula has contacts in Boston, just like I suspected. She knows Miss Zenobia is deep in spellwork with her friend Agnes Potter. She said Miss Zenobia isn't even entirely *in* this dimension. We'd never reach her in time."

"We should try," Debra said and attempted to wrench Patricia's hand off hers.

"No, Patricia is right," Linda said, wand in hand. "It's up to us."

"We can do this," Patricia said as Debra still clutched the telephone, fear and doubt written all over her.

"But they're older than us," Debra said.

"Older, but out of training," Patricia said. Which was a lie, given what my mother had just been saying. "They went back to mundane lives, all three of them. They don't have what we have. They turned their back on their calling."

"Listen!" Linda cried. The library windows were wide open, the heavy July air smotheringly still. The shouts were faint but were clearly coming from the backyard. "Come on!"

Debra looked grim, but drew her wand all the same. The three of them ran out of the library and down the back steps to the kitchen and then out into the yard. The bouncing of the turquoise on Patricia's chest made this hard to follow, but I caught enough glimpses to fill in their route from my own memories of the school.

They drew to a halt in the orchard, and the necklace was once more lying still. Our mothers were there fighting some unseen foe, firing shots from the wands at a common point in the sky.

"They're attacking the bridge!" Patricia shouted to the others. With her power, she could see the time portal, but her necklace could not.

Suddenly a woman's screams rent the air. I knew that woman's voice. I had heard it before. It was Miss Zenobia's sister, Juno.

"Stop it!" Patricia shrieked at them, then ran to get between our mothers and the point I knew to be the anchor point of the bridge across time. She spread her arms and legs as wide as she could.

"Get out of the way," my mother snarled.

"No," Patricia said. "I won't let you."

"It has to be done," my mother said.

"Can't you see what you're destroying is more than a mere bridge? Can't you hear its pain?" Patricia all but wailed.

The fierce look in my mother's eyes was undiminished. 'It has to be done," she said again. "Step aside."

"No," Patricia said.

All three of our mothers struck her at once. Bolts of power danced over the surface of the necklace, and we could hear Patricia crying out in pain. Then she was flat on her back, staring up at the sky. All we could see were streaky white clouds high in a washed-out blue sky.

"Give it up," Marie said. "We have more power than you. You can't win."

"We can't just let you do this," Patricia said. Our view tilted, as if she were pushing herself up on her elbows.

"I've explained this to you so many times, but you just won't listen," my mother said.

"You've abandoned your calling!" Patricia said. Linda and Debra came into view, flanking her with wands at the ready, trying very hard not to look scared.

"And I told you why," my mother said, but Lula spoke up before she could say more.

"We've already tried arguing this out with the kids," she said. "Time is short, but we were almost there. Didn't you feel it? We need to bring it down now. For good."

Then a lot of things happened all at once. The next several minutes were very hard to parse. I knew I was watching magical combat, but without seeing it through a witch's eyes, most of what was happening was invisible and frankly inscrutable. Was this what Edward and Otto had seen when we had fought the coven before? This chaos of gestures and shouts and people flickering in and out of reality?

And that screaming. Wherever Juno was, the turquoise necklace couldn't see, but her cries of pain filled the orchard. What must the neighbors be thinking?

Our mothers did seem to have more raw power than Patricia and her friends, but shooting bolts from their wands was the largest part of their magic. It was enough to keep the three pinned down at the foot of the bridge, but not enough to make them abandon their post.

"We can't beat them," Debra said. "They're too strong. We can't even advance on them."

"Worse than that," Patricia said. "They are still attacking the time bridge. I know you two can't feel what I do, but it's bad. Really bad. A couple more hits and I don't think there'll be anything left to protect."

"What can we do?" Debra asked.

"Linda, smokescreen," Patricia said. Linda nodded, biting her lip as she swept her arm, hand and wand over the orchard between them and our mothers with a theatrical wave.

"That's only going to last a minute," she said, although I couldn't quite see what she had done.

"I only need a minute," Patricia said. She turned to face the back wall and dropped to sit on the ground. I could hear a change in her breathing. I was pretty sure she had just gone to the world of threads.

"Hurry, hurry, hurry," Debra was whispering over and over.

"They know it's a glamour," Linda whispered back. "They know we're still here. They're going to blast the entire yard with everything they have left. There's no way they aren't going to hit us."

Then Patricia sat up straighter with a deep sucking in of air.

"Did you do it?" Debra asked.

"It's done," Patricia said. "None of them have time magic. They'll never find it now."

"Down!" Linda cried, and there was another moment of loud chaos and screams. Patricia must have fallen to her belly on the ground because the necklace's memory went all black.

Then it was silent.

We could hear Patricia breathing hard. Then she was sitting up, and we saw Debra and Linda bent forward with their hands on their knees, also breathing hard.

Then she looked up at our mothers. Lula was bleeding from her nose and one of her ears. Marie had lost her wand, head swiveling as she attempted to find it before the others could. My mother looked exceedingly pale, clutching her swollen belly and breathing as if through a contraction.

"Are you okay?" Patricia asked.

My mother tried to bark out a sharp laugh between breaths but didn't quite pull it off.

"What did you do?" Lula demanded.

"I moved the anchor point for the bridge," Patricia said. "It doesn't go anywhere anymore. You can't force it to take you anywhere. You can't change time; I made sure of that. The timeline is quite safe. Which is more than I can say for you three if you're still here when Miss Zenobia gets back."

"She'll be just," Debra said. "If you ask for forgiveness, I'm sure she'll give it to you."

My mother barked another laugh but shook her head.

"What do we do now?" Marie asked. "She's right. What I'm sensing of the bridge, the other end is whipping around like a dropped firehose."

"We failed," Lula said. "We have to run."

My mother stopped her controlled breathing and straightened her back, throwing her hair back out of her eyes. Then she lifted one foot and looked under it to see what she was standing on. It was Marie's wand. She bent awkwardly to retrieve it and toss it to Marie, who snatched it out of the air with ease.

"We have to run," my mother agreed, but she was raising her own wand, past the point of aiming it at Patricia, sweeping it up into the air. "But first we should cover our tracks."

"Hold on to me!" Patricia cried, twisting one way and then the other to catch hold of Debra and Linda.

There was an explosion of sound and fury, and then there was black silence.

The three witches across from us were opening their eyes and releasing each other's hands.

"I pulled us onto the bridge," Patricia said. "We left our own time behind. It was the only way to save ourselves."

"But it was at such a cost," Debra said, fussing over the further weakened Patricia.

CHAPTER 16

"You want us to believe that our mothers were evil?" I asked. I was annoyed. Nothing we had seen had given us any clue as to what had happened to our mothers in the years between. How had they ended up in the 90s? The last thing we knew about them was still the photographs from the news story.

"I never said evil," Patricia said. "Just misguided. You were surely watching closely as the spell unfurled. You know it was not fake or doctored or in any way a lie."

I looked at Brianna, who gave the smallest of nods. "It is true as far as it goes," she said. "Clearly we're missing some context."

"I wasn't always wearing that particular piece, so I can't show you everything, but I can tell you," Patricia said. "Your mothers were older than us. We looked up to them. They had such power, such potential. You know, most of the charm school students weren't even witches, and most of the ones who were witches had little interest in pursuing a life of magic. For we three, who wanted to master magic more than anything, the casual way your mothers just threw all that aside was heartbreaking for us."

"That's your context?" I asked.

"Let me finish," Patricia said. "There was a time I was close with your mother, Amanda. Kathleen was like the older sister I never had. She taught me so much when I was young. But she never cared for time magic, and when I started to discover the nature of my power, she didn't know what to make of it all. She quizzed me over and over. What did I see? What had I done? She was so paranoid, and yet of what, I had no idea. It was when she was about fourteen that she and Marie and Lula started spending all their time together. They hung out in the back of the library and wouldn't share what they were doing with anyone. Always they spoke in whispers, always they glared warnings at anyone who accidentally happened upon them."

"Our mothers were a bad influence?" Sophie asked with a raised brow.

"I don't know," Patricia said, clutching her hands together in a show of sincerity. "I really don't. There was definitely *a* bad influence, but I don't know where exactly it came from. In a house full of magic, it could've come from anywhere."

"Are you sure you're not the paranoid one?" I asked.

"No, listen," Patricia said. "They started to have doubts about Miss Zenobia. They avoided her, in her own school! It wasn't unusual for girls with magical skills to leave the charm school without pursuing their craft, as I've said, but I don't think that's what they did. Oh, they told Miss Zenobia that was what they were doing. But I don't think they were choosing a normal life over a magical one. I think they were already running away from Miss Zenobia."

"Why?" I asked.

"I wish I knew," Patricia sighed. "I wish I knew why they turned on her like they did."

"But my mother said she'd explained it to you," I said.

"That was all babblings," Patricia said. "None of it made any sense. That's why she seemed like a paranoid to me. She was afraid of every-thing, and for no apparent reason. I mean, I know you three barely know Miss Zenobia. She was stern and demanding as a teacher, but she would certainly never harm any of us."

I desperately wanted to ask if they knew where Miss Zenobia was now, but I didn't want to tip our hand. Still, if there was another way to get at the same question...

"So Miss Zenobia never came back to rescue you when you fell backward through time?" Sophie asked, and I gave a mental cheer that she had read my mind.

"She tried," Patricia said. "I could feel her when she got home, even across time. I sensed her trying to mend what your mothers had destroyed. She pinned the bridge down, even. On both ends. That had never happened before. There had always been an anchor point in her present, but the other end had been random. Now it wasn't. Now it led straight back to us. I could feel it."

"But she didn't cross it," Sophie said.

Patricia shook her head.

"And neither did you?" I asked.

It may sound strange, but at that moment I was very aware of Patricia, Linda and Debra not trading glances. I felt that lack. I was certain that what came next would be at least in part a lie.

"What I did, moving the anchor point so that those without time magic couldn't find it, it was a strain. For a long time, I felt broken. I wasn't sure I'd ever be able to use time magic again."

"Then I came into your life," I said.

"Yes, but then you did just what your mother did," Patricia said, blinking back tears. "You destroyed the bridge. Didn't you hear the screams?"

"I did," I said. "I even know what they are. Who they are. Do you?"

Patricia's eyes widened. Again, I didn't think she was feigning emotion, but how could I ever know for sure?

"No, I don't think you do," I said with more certainty than I felt.

"You destroyed the bridge, and we three are still trapped here," she said.

"I didn't destroy the bridge, obviously," I said with a dismissive wave. "You can see for yourselves the three of us are right here, not in our time."

"I suspected as much," she said. "There was something I could almost sense, but never quite. That's why we had to get your attention. To bring you back."

"We're not bringing you to our time," Sophie said.

"We don't want to go to your time," she said. "We want to go back to our time."

"That's not how it works," I said.

"That's not how it works *now*," Patricia said. "But it worked differently before. It could work any way we want it to if we shape it together."

"We just want to go home," Debra said. "Put us where we belong, then close the door behind us. We'll never trouble you again."

"You'll still be in our past," Sophie said. "You'll still be able to hurt us in a way we couldn't defend from."

"We won't," Patricia said.

"How can we trust that?" Sophie asked. "How can we trust you?"

"I don't know why you even have to," Patricia said. Even sitting as she was, she started to slump over, and Linda put in arm around her to support her. "You don't have to trust me, because if I make a single step out of line, your friend here can end me. She knows it. You know it. So how does trust enter into it?"

"I have some questions," I said before Sophie could continue arguing with her. Sophie threw up her hands in frustration, but let me talk.

"Ask me anything," Patricia said.

"Who is your employer?" I asked. "You and Evanora have dodged this question every time. You're going to answer it now."

"We don't *have* an employer," Patricia said, sounding annoyed. "We're not employed."

"But you aren't free agents either, are you?" I asked.

There it was again, that feeling of them not trading glances. Was I sensing some sort of telepathy between them? Or was I just that paranoid now?

"Every coven has a focal point," Brianna said. "An ideal they work to bring into the world, sometimes. More often, a god or entity they serve. Whom or what do you serve?"

Patricia started to swoon, and Linda and Debra both fussed over her, but this was surely fake. She was buying herself just a little bit of time to figure out how she was going to evade this question yet again.

"We do serve... an entity," she said, to my surprise. Then she brushed Linda and Debra away so she could push herself back up to a seated position. "We do. But the nature of that entity has always been a mystery to me. To all three of us. Well, all thirteen of us."

"You must have chosen something to summon," Brianna said.

"No, it found us," she said. "Not long after we came here, the three of us alone and lost in time. It spoke to us. Getting us home was beyond what it was willing to do for us, but that didn't mean it couldn't help us to help ourselves. We gained in power. It helped us attract the others, many of them across other portals of time. We all serve the same master, and yet none of us know its true name or nature."

"You fools," Brianna said.

"Our eyes are open," Patricia said. "The contract between us is fair. We've gained so much. I mean, look!" She threw her arms up, encompassing the massive height of the tower we were standing in. "All this! It's beyond imagining what we can now do. And it asks so little of us in return."

"Like what?" Sophie asked. "What does it demand from you?"

"It's not even like that," Patricia said. "It just guides us to what we must do to take the next step."

"Like what?" Sophie asked again, distinctly articulating each syllable this time.

"Well, lately the only thing it asks of me is that I take Amanda on as an apprentice. I failed at that once before, but it wasn't angry with me. It knows these sorts of journeys require a lot of steps, and sometimes there are false starts."

"Why would I be your apprentice if, as you say, I am far more powerful than you?" I asked.

"You have power," she conceded. "But I have knowledge. I know the structure the time bridge had before Miss Zenobia fixed both ends. With your power and my knowledge, we can restore it to what it was."

"And that's what your master wants?" Brianna asked.

"That's what *we* want," Patricia said. "All my master wants is for Amanda and me to work together."

"To what aim?" I asked.

"To free us from this time, I'm sure," she said, but there was something about her careless shrug I didn't like. "Look, this is the bargain we're looking for. You help me to fix the time portal and get the three of us back to our proper time. That's it. In return, I make one phone call, and your friend and all his relatives will be restored. And I'll make that phone call before we even get started, as a measure of good faith."

Sophie snorted, but I held up a hand.

"And Jackson?"

"And what?" Patricia asked, blinking.

"Jackson, the little boy. Jackson Smith." She just kept blinking at me; it was infuriating. "I don't know if he was a first attempt that didn't sufficiently grab my attention or a test subject or what. But you have to put him back."

"I'm sorry, Amanda. I honestly don't know what you're talking about," she said. "We were very careful when we chose your friend Nick as a target. We spent a lot of time going over just how to do it. We had to be sure we could put it back, or it would be no good. Don't you see? It wouldn't be leverage if we couldn't make it go to either outcome, depending on how you responded."

I could feel Sophie and Brianna's eyes on me. They were lending me support and what strength they could, but they were leaving the actual decision up to me.

"I need time," I said. "This is huge, and I can't make a decision on a whim."

Patricia looked like she was personally disappointed in me, but worked hard to summon up a smile. "Take time," she said. "But not a lot of it. As you can probably see, I don't have a lot of time left. But I guess you don't care about that. But you should know if you wait too long, we might not be able to undo what we did. Your friend Nick will be lost forever."

"I don't need a lot of time," I said, getting up from the floor. "Meet us at dawn in the back orchard at the charm school. I'll give you my answer there."

Clearly, that location pleased her immensely, as a huge grin spread across her face.

"Dawn. At the school," she said. She looked like she wanted to shake on it, but I wasn't interested in letting her touch me. I turned and left the tower, Brianna and Sophie on either side of me, matching my stride.

Either Patricia's glee was filling that entire hollow tower, or I was feeling the presence of that thing she served, whatever it was.

I'm not sure which idea creeped me out more.

e went back through the wall, an experience just as horrifying as the first time, then picked our way down the alley of slimy cobblestones towards the comforting streetlight that stood on the sidewalk we had left behind what felt like hours before.

When we reached it and saw not a single car moving through the quiet streets of St. Paul in the dead of night, we realized it had been hours. It was closer to dawn than midnight, but not so close that even milkmen were stirring yet.

Worse, it was snowing like mad. If we ended up walking back to the school, we were clearly going to regret our choices in footwear.

"Now what?" Brianna asked, looking up and down the street for any sign of motion among the parked cars. I looked higher, at the buildings around us, but not a single lighted window broke the swirling snow and darkness.

Then Sophie moved to lean against the lamppost to adjust her shoe, and the moment the glittering red of her dress caught the light, we all heard the roar of a car engine coming to life. We pulled out our wands, hoping it was Otto, but not willing to bet on it.

The car pulled up to the curb in front of us, and the shadowy figure inside leaned across the front seat to heave the passenger door open.

It was Benny, Otto's young protégé. "Get in!" he said, waving for us to hurry. We piled inside, and he gunned the accelerator before we quite had the doors closed.

"We're not being chased, Benny," I said. "We're safe for the moment."

"Otto told you to watch for us?" Sophie asked, leaning over the back of the front seat.

"Yeah," Benny said. "He said he had to stay with Edward, but that you might need a ride. Sorry, I think I dozed off a bit. The sound of the snow hitting the windscreen was just too hypnotic. I hope you weren't waiting long?"

"You were just in time," I said.

"We're not going to Edward's, though," Sophie said. "We need to get straight to the charm school."

"Got it," Benny said and jammed down the accelerator again.

If it had been Otto who had picked us up, I'm sure at that moment we'd already be discussing everything that had happened and what to do next, but with young Benny in the car, that was impossible. But without talking about that, there was nothing else to say.

So we drove in silence save for the whistling of the wind through the partly opened windows and the sound of snowflakes hitting the windscreen. It *was* hypnotic. But then I hadn't had a full night's sleep in quite some time.

Benny had us at the school in record time.

"Should I wait here?" he asked as we climbed out of the car.

"No," Sophie said. "We don't know how long we'll be."

"Tell Edward," I started to say, but didn't know how to finish. What could I tell him that could safely travel through Benny? I couldn't say we'd gone back to the present or that he was safe from the witches.

And I couldn't say that I was working as hard as I could to find an end to everything where we were together.

"Tell Edward and Otto we got home safe," Sophie said, grabbing my arm to steer me up the walk to the back garden.

Despite all of Patricia's assurances, I still did all my usual checks for interference or magical traps before pulling the three of us back through the wormhole.

Doing that bit of magic had given me a charge, but the moment we were in 2019, all the weariness of the long day and night dropped back down on me. And yet there was no time to rest. I trudged after Brianna and Sophie, into the house and up to the library.

"Where do we start?" I asked as I dropped into my chair at the table.

"I wish we could start with sleep," Sophie said. "Maybe coffee is in order?"

"Time is short," Brianna said. Then she came to stand behind me. Her fingertips touched my temples, and I tried to twist away. "Hold still. This will help," she said.

I had never had a reason not to trust her, so I sat still. She whispered a few guttural words, then lifted her hands away from my head.

I didn't see a brain fog being pulled out of my head, but the feeling was much the same. My mind was clear and alert. Even my body stopped complaining about how much it wanted to lie down.

"Neat trick," I said as she circled around the table to do the same to Sophie.

I watched Sophie transform from late-stage dark-circles-under-the-eyes exhaustion to bright alertness in the blink of an eye.

"Is this what you do in place of sleeping?" I asked.

"Oh, no," Brianna said after touching her own temples. "You'll know why tomorrow night. This is strictly temporary, and we'll be paying for it later. But it felt necessary."

"First thing," I said, "do we believe what she showed us about our mothers?"

"So far as it goes, yes," Brianna said. "But it's a fair assumption that she chose what to show us carefully."

"And removed the context," Sophie added.

"What we learned that we didn't already know is mere details," Brianna said. "We already knew they fought over control of the time portal and that our mothers nearly destroyed it. We still don't know why, or what happened afterward."

"They showed us something they thought would win our trust," I said. "I guess we're in agreement that we still don't feel that trust."

"Definitely not," Sophie said. Brianna was shaking her head emphatically.

"I'm operating from the position that we don't know what Patricia really wants," I said. "But what she's asking for is the same as before. For me to work with her. Because the sort of time magic she wants to do involves two time witches."

"And the last time she said that's what she wanted, she promptly attacked you on the other side," Sophie said.

"Well, to be fair, I had refused to do what she wanted," I said. "For all I know, something different would have happened had I agreed."

"Don't tell me you believe that?" Sophie said.

"No, but just to be fair," I said with a shrug.

"Yeah, well, that brings us to the point where they think they're the good guys and weren't sure if we were the bad guys," Brianna said.

"That's obviously crazy talk," I said. "Good guys don't use the methods they've been employing."

"Agreed," Sophie said.

"Who knows what they went through when they first found themselves in the 1920s? Teenagers, on their own in a strange world," Brianna said.

"It can't have been more than a few months to look at them," Sophie said.

"Still, we don't know. Maybe it literally is crazy talk," Brianna said.

"I don't think we're qualified to give them a full mental evaluation," Sophie said. "Maybe we're not even qualified to judge them morally either. Does it matter whether we decide they're actually bad guys, or confused good guys using iffy techniques, or whatever?"

"We need to do whatever it takes to get Nick and Jackson back," I said. "That's where I think our focus has to be."

"What if that means putting even more lives at risk?" Brianna asked.

I wanted to say something dismissive, but I couldn't. She was right. It wouldn't be worth that.

"Here's another thing," Sophie said. "Their employer or entity or whatever."

"Yes, that's the biggest problem," Brianna said.

"Do you know anything about that sort of thing?" I asked.

"Only the basics," she said. "The coven my mother belonged to was organized around a set of principles, not a specific goddess or being or whatever. And there were very specific reasons for doing that. The sorts of things that want covens to serve them and revere them, they may put on a benign face, but that's often a lie."

"This thing Patricia spoke of, that offered unlimited power and asked so little in return," Sophie said. "That really sounds like a con."

"Yes," Brianna said. "But I can't tell if they honestly believe that this thing they serve means them well or if they are in on the con."

"Either way, they're looking to bring trouble down on us," Sophie said. "I wish we could just walk away from all of this. Destroy what's left of the portal, leave them in the past, and just walk away."

"But we can't," I said. "They can destroy everyone we know and love, and we'll be defenseless to stop them."

"They came into 1927 from our time bridge," Brianna said. "It feels like they are our responsibility."

Silence fell on the library as we each lapsed into our own thoughts. I wished mine were more coherent. My heart ached at the loss of Nick and Jackson; I had to put that right.

And I had to get back to Edward.

"She said she would restore Nick before I went into the world of threads with her. She'd prove it first," I said.

"And we're going to trust that?" Sophie asked.

"No," I said. "One of us will have to be here to see that it's done and send word back to me before I do anything."

"How are we going to do that?" Brianna asked. "Send word, I mean. Communicate across time."

"One of us will be here in 2019 to confirm, one of us in 1928 to receive the message and send it to me," I said. "We're meeting at the school and there's a phone there. Otto's people might be able to confirm the broken couple was reunited, but that's not good enough for me. I need someone with eyes on Nick before I do anything."

"But that still means you'll be in their clutches alone," Sophie said. "I don't like that."

"I don't like it either, but do you see another way?" I asked.

"What about that boy, Jackson?" Brianna asked. "She keeps denying she even knows him."

"Maybe she doesn't," I said. "Maybe he's some side effect of what she did. I hope he'll be restored when Nick is, but if he isn't... well, the next thing I'll be doing is going into the world of threads. I can sort it out from there, I think. Certainly, if I'm there with Patricia, I will know for a fact if she's responsible or not."

"What are you going to do if she attacks you again?" Sophie asked. "With no backup? We had to carry you out of there last time. You only survived because the four of us were there."

"I feel certain I'm going to be okay," I said. "I'm so much stronger now than before. And she's so much weaker."

"That could be an illusion," Brianna said. "They might even be allowing us to see through the other glamours so that we'll believe that this one is real. Our power might not have grown as much as we think."

"I don't see another way out of this," I said. "And I know I can do this."

"Can we address the other elephant in the room?" Sophie asked.

"What elephant?" I asked.

"Your..." Sophie began, ending with a vague hand gesture that failed to summon the word she was looking for.

"Hubris," Brianna said for her.

"Exactly. Hubris," Sophie said. "I may not have read a lot of Greek myths, but I've read enough to know that hubris is never a good thing. And while we were out of town, you've broken out in an epic case of it."

"I haven't," I said. "I've gained some power and skill, but I worked for that. My confidence in my abilities is matched by my actual abilities. You've seen what I can do with the wormhole in the backyard."

"It's not just that," Brianna said.

"It's the secrecy and callous rule-breaking," Sophie said. "You lied to us on every conference call about what you were up to. Why?"

"You didn't need to know," I said. "I didn't want you both flying back here before you had finished what you'd left town to do. So I hid a few things. But like I keep telling you, I was careful."

"It really does seem like adolescent behavior," Brianna said, not quite looking at me. "The fact that you can't see that even now is troubling."

"This isn't one of your compulsions, is it?" Sophie asked. I could tell by the tone of her voice that she knew that it wasn't. I shook my head.

"Is it something else?" Brianna asked earnestly. "That fight on the time bridge nearly destroyed Patricia. Did it harm you as well? Or just change you in some way? I felt other entities lurking, watching. Like other things were invested in the outcome."

"The time bridge was infused with Juno's essence and power," I said.

"It wasn't just that," Brianna said.

"There was something else," Sophie said. "Maybe this entity Patricia spoke of, although I never sensed it reaching out to help her. But maybe it reached out to you?"

"You think I've been turned or something?" I asked.

They both thought that over for far longer than I found comfortable before looking at each other and saying, "no."

"We're just worried," Sophie said. "Are you absolutely sure that all of this is coming from you? Are you sure, really sure, that you can do what Patricia asks and be safe?"

I bit back a glib answer. Her concern was palpable.

I had been doing whatever I wanted because I was confident I could get away with it. I guess hubris was a good word for that.

I closed my eyes and slipped into the world of threads. But rather than examine the world around me, I shifted my attention to my own self.

That was tricky. I was outside of my body, but what I wanted to see wasn't part of my physical body. But I had managed this once before, after Patricia had attacked me and left my threads in tattered shreds. I knew I could do it again, but it was still a challenge.

When I was finally able to bring it into focus, I was in awe.

I glowed with power. Far more than what I could explain with the magic I had been practicing. Where had I accumulated that? Had it come from the fight when I destroyed the bridge?

I looked for any sign of, literally, any strings attached to my power or my skills. But there were none.

I opened my eyes to find both Sophie and Brianna watching me anxiously.

"I can do it," I said, but soberly this time.

They still looked skeptical, but neither said a word. They were ready to concede, but only because there were no other options, really.

But I had more to say. "Have you ever wondered why Miss Zenobia turned over her sole charge as ward of this portal to the three of us? I mean, why three?"

"We were young and untried," Sophie guessed.

"It had something to do with our mothers," Brianna said. "They were all gone, but we were what was left. I guess she couldn't pick just one of us."

"Maybe," I said. "But maybe it's because of just this thing we're about to do."

"What do you mean?" Sophie asked. "That she foresaw this?"

"No, I don't think this exactly," I said. "But something like this. Maybe she knew at some point we'd have to do something major across time. Something that would involve one of us in the past, one of us in the present, and one of us standing outside of time."

But of course, there was no way for us to know for sure. I don't think we'd ever once succeeded in figuring out what Miss Zenobia had been thinking.

But when we got up from the table, I was no longer the only one confident we were doing the right thing.

CHAPTER 18

I left my cellphone with Brianna in 2019. When Nick was restored, she should see his name reappear in my contacts. Then she could call him to hear his voice.

Getting word to Sophie and me in 1928 would be a bit trickier. The other way across time was easier. We could just leave a written message lying around, and one of the 1928 students we couldn't see would put it into one of the many dated files that were eventually kept in Mr. Trevor's office.

But to deliver a message against the flow of time, Brianna would have to contact the witch Tabitha in England. Tabitha was the ward of another time portal and could go back to 1928 and send a telegram to the school that would be left out until we saw it.

I wasn't a fan of that plan. I wanted to just dart back to the present and talk to Nick myself, but Sophie and Brianna nixed that idea. The less Patricia saw of my magic, the better. I could see the sense in this.

But still, I really hated I wasn't going to hear Nick's voice myself. If Patricia was who she said she was and wanted what she said she wanted, there would be no problem. But if she was trying to play us, I was going to have to take down the time portal for good. And if that was how everything ended, I fully intended to be standing in 1928 when it was all over.

Not getting a chance to speak to Nick again was the one part of that plan that I really didn't like. But at least he would be alive.

Sophie and I flowed through the wormhole to 1928 to find that the thickly falling snow from before was now a proper blizzard. The sun was rising somewhere, unseen behind the cloud cover.

Sophie and I quickly ran into the school to watch for Patricia to arrive from the humid warmth of the solarium. It was strange standing in all of that lush greenery, the smell of herbs thick in the air, and watching the snow driving coldly against the thick glass all around us.

"I don't like you facing her alone," Sophie said.

"I don't either," I said. "But it helps to know you'll be close, and you can summon Brianna too if need be."

"For all the good we'd do," Sophie said. "Neither of us can even perceive the time portal now, let alone use it without you."

That thought hadn't occurred to me. "Are you worried about getting trapped here?" I asked.

"Yes," Sophie said without hesitation. "Your confidence better not be misplaced."

There was nothing I could say that would be any more persuasive than what I said before.

But maybe there was something I could do.

I reached up and unclasped Cynthia's amulet from around my neck, then pressed it into Sophie's palm.

"Take it," I said. "Just in case. Miss Zenobia's magic was stronger than anyone's. It will get you home, no matter how changed the portal is."

Sophie looked like she was going to refuse it, but then closed her hand over it and slipped it into her coat pocket. "Thanks. I like 1928, but my life is in 2019."

"Antoine?" I guessed. "Did you see him when you were in New Orleans?"

"Briefly. He came home for spring break for a few days," she said.

"You've talked to him since?" I asked. "I mean, since you came home? But then I guess if I remember him, he couldn't have been erased."

"No, he's fine," Sophie said. "We exchange texts every couple of hours. I think he's amused I'm suddenly so chatty. It's not like I'm going to tell him why I need to keep hearing from him. I can't wait for this all to be over."

"It won't be long now," I said, and even as the words were out of my mouth, I saw the outlines of three figures emerging from the layers of blowing snow. As they drew closer, I could see Patricia in the middle, struggling through the deep snow. Debra had an arm around her to support her while Linda walked a little way ahead, breaking up a path through the banked snow, partly with her booted feet and partly with blasts of heat from the end of her wand.

They came up the steps of the back porch and let themselves in the back door as if they were completely at home. Which I guess they were.

"Is this weather magic?" Sophie asked before they'd even pushed back their hoods.

"If it is, it isn't from us," Debra said.

"It won't affect what we're about to do," Patricia said. She sounded winded, and I wondered just how far they had walked. All the way from the tower?

"We aren't about to do anything until my friend is back among the living," I said. "You promised proof."

"Just let me use the telephone," Patricia said and headed into the kitchen. Debra and Linda settled into the wrought-iron chairs in the solarium to wait, but Sophie and I followed Patricia into the kitchen. She dialed a number from memory, then looked to us as she waited for someone on the other end to answer, putting a muffling hand over the mouthpiece. "I suppose you know how Alice kept the couple in question apart?"

"Judicious application of fruit punch, I believe," I said.

Patricia nodded. "But she's befriended them both since. She's been talking Robert up to Dorothy since the dance. Now all she has to do is give Robert a nudge." She took her hand off the mouthpiece of the phone to speak into it. "Alice? It's time."

Then she hung up.

"Well?" I said.

"You heard me. It's done. It's time for you to hold up your end of the bargain," she said.

"You promised proof," I said.

"How long is it going to take for him to come back?" Sophie asked. "If this Alice has to talk to Robert, then Robert has to talk to Dorothy. Even after all that is done, how long will it be until Nick's existence is assured?"

"It doesn't matter," Patricia said. "It could take decades, and it would still have happened in time."

I looked to the cork message board next to the phone and found a slip of paper I was sure I hadn't seen there before. It was a telegram from Tabitha in London, relaying a message from Brianna.

HAVE SPOKEN WITH NICK. HE IS WITH ME NOW. HE DOESN'T REMEMBER JACKSON.

I bit my lip but handed the telegram to Sophie wordlessly. Patricia moved to read over her shoulder.

"I did what I said I would," Patricia said. "I swear to you, I don't know who this Jackson person is. It's nothing to do with me."

"What do you think?" Sophie asked me, acting as if Patricia weren't even there.

"I think I'll be able to see the truth of the matter the moment I'm in the world of threads," I said, then turned to Patricia. "I know some things about Jackson and his connection to this time. If I see any of that leading back to you, our deal is off."

"Fine," she spat back. "But we have to act now."

"Why the hurry? I would think with time magic there would never be any rush," Sophie said.

"That shows how little you know of time magic," Patricia said angrily. But she didn't seem to have the energy to maintain that anger and deflated before our eyes. "I'm not well. The time portal might be able to wait for all eternity to be restored, but I cannot."

"Repairing the time portal is going to heal you?" I asked.

"I need to get back to my own time," Patricia said. "All three of us do. I can heal there."

Sophie's eyes were narrowed with suspicion, and I knew just what she was picturing. A suddenly revived Patricia turning on me the moment she had the power to do so.

"Then let's get you home," I said to Patricia. I gave Sophie a look I hoped said I was prepared for anything, but the grim set of her face didn't relax at all.

"I'm going out to the orchard with you," Sophie said. "If Debra and Linda are going to be there, I will be too."

"I have no objection," Patricia said.

"Like I'd care if you did," Sophie grumbled under her breath.

The five of us tromped through the drifted snow to the orchard near the back wall of the garden. The snow-laden wind cut less like a knife and more like a chainsaw, the flakes of icy snow peppering my exposed cheeks painfully. But the trees protected us from the worst of it once we were standing among them.

Linda and Debra huddled close to Patricia, speaking a last few words to each other. I settled down on the snow and started controlling my breathing, but I could feel Sophie standing behind me, ready to back me up.

More, even without going into the world of threads, I could feel Brianna standing in the exact same spot, ninety-one years in the future. She too was prepared to support me, although she couldn't sense the wormhole without my help any more than Sophie could. But she was making herself open. I could draw on her power if I needed it, just as I could from Sophie.

I felt safe and secure, anchored in both times. Patricia would not be so well grounded as I.

At last Debra and Linda fell back and Patricia sat down on the snow before me, also cross-legged, our knees not quite touching.

"How shall we do this?" I asked.

"We need to be on opposite ends of the bridge to repair it," Patricia said. "I'll stay here on this end; you go back to your end and reach out to me."

"No," I said. "You're going to 2019. I'll stay here."

"But I can't pass through the portal since you collapsed it," she said.

"I'll move you through," I said.

"I don't see the point of doing it that way, but as you like it," Patricia said with a careless shrug. Then she closed her eyes, and we both shifted our awareness.

I was immediately on my guard, grasping at the threads around me, moving to protect my physical form but also to catch hold of what was left of the time portal to shut it down completely with one quick move.

But no attack came. Patricia was just there, waiting for me to move her through the portal. I could see that she sensed it near her, but she couldn't quite get a bead on it.

I started to reach for her, but doubt held me back. I had changed up her initial plan because I didn't trust her, but what if going to 2019 had been her intent all along? Was she out-thinking me? Was this the trap?

I looked at her carefully. She was indeed not well. She looked like she was consuming herself from within, using her magical reserves to keep her body alive. And her time had definitely grown short. But I couldn't see the cause. What was making her so ill?

I redirected my attention to my own body, and the stuffed rabbit still tucked away in my pocket. The threads that ran towards the house next door and towards Edward's apartment a block away were, if anything, even fainter than before. But nothing connected to Patricia.

I guess she hadn't been lying to me about that.

Remembering that Brianna had sensed some other presence in our last fight in the time portal, I reached out with my own feelings. Aside from Juno, who always lurked within the structure of the portal itself, I felt no one but Patricia and me.

I could, however, feel Patricia's impatience with my caution. Not that I cared; I would delay forever if I had to.

But there was nothing else to be done. I took hold of Patricia's threads and fed them through the wormhole, streaming her through to the other side.

I felt her regain form on the other side. I also felt Brianna's sudden awareness that she was not alone in 2019. She had her wand in hand, waiting for any sign that she would have to use it.

But Patricia just turned her attention back to me and to the time portal that stood between us.

I reached out to her and she to me, and between us, our power began to soak into the bridge itself. It expanded faster than a thirsty sponge under a spray of water, growing back to its full awe-inspiring size. I could hear Juno, but not screaming this time. The sound was more like sighs of relief.

This wasn't even hard. The magic flowed through me and did exactly as I wanted it to, as if I had been doing this all my life. I could still feel Brianna and Sophie. They couldn't sense me, though. They weren't sure whether or not to be worried that I wasn't drawing from them. I tried to send them a single thought, that all was going well. I think they got it, but I only spared them that one thought before returning to the work on the time bridge.

We brought it to the point where it had been when I had first been aware of it, but Patricia kept on feeding me power. Then I felt something in my mind, some sort of telepathic signal. It wasn't like someone talking to me; it was more like I just suddenly knew something I had never been taught.

I started spinning off the power, creating little side ramps off the main bridge. I thought I was only forming one, the one needed to take Patricia, Debra and Linda back to 1968, but what I was seeing was dozens of them growing off the bridge like the hairs on the back of a caterpillar, bristling out to dozens of different times, forming permanent connections with each.

What was the purpose of this?

But I didn't have to know that to know that Patricia was trying to get more out of our bargain than I had agreed to. I changed what I was doing, stopping the flow of power from Patricia and me into the bridge. Then I broke off my connection with Patricia and began to draw everything back out of the bridge, back into myself.

I really should have asked myself how Patricia—poor, frail Patricia —had been able to send so much power into me. I guess the beauty of what we had been creating had blinded me. The flow of magic through her to me and through me to the time portal itself had just felt so right. Like I had waited all my life to do what I was doing now.

But I hadn't even noticed that her strength had grown to match my own. Not until I tried to cut her off from that power.

This time, when she moved to sever me from the rest of the world, she moved with superhuman speed. Every thread that held me within the flow of time was cut in one deadly swipe of her magic. She had learned from her first failure.

And I had woefully underestimated her.

I reached out for everything, for my anchor points in the past and present, for the bridge itself. I sensed briefly Brianna standing in the present, Nick at her side. I sensed Sophie in 1928, and Otto and Edward were with her. But none of them could help me now.

Neither could the bridge. Even as I reached for it, I felt Patricia's power flowing through it, claiming it in a way I would never have thought to do myself.

Then I could feel nothing around me at all. I was in nothingness. I *was* nothingness. Was I dying or dead already?

How long would I go on like this?

But just before despair could take me, something pulled me out of that nothingness.

Or rather, someone.

Juno.

CHAPTER 19

Something was tickling my nose.

I was lying on the ground, face up to a brilliant blue sky, with the sound of gurgling water somewhere not too far away. The sun was warm on my body. Perhaps too warm; my face was starting to get that tight, about to have a sunburn feeling. The smell of springtime grass all around me was comforting. I hadn't smelled it since I had moved to St. Paul, but it had always surrounded me back in the little town in Iowa where I had grown up.

Then a breeze danced over me, and the blade of grass bending over my head started tickling me again. I brushed it away and sat up.

Where was I?

I could see nothing but grass, but I didn't smell any cows. The water sound was definitely coming from a largish stream off to my right somewhere beyond the waves of grass.

I closed my eyes, shifting at once to the world of webs.

The usual dense interconnectedness was completely changed. The nodes were fewer, the threads not so bright. Everything was streamlined, minimalist even. What did this mean?

I was just opening my eyes when I heard the sound of something rustling through the tall grass, rustling ever closer to me. I turned to see a woman heading my way, a woman wearing a white sheath dress belted at the waist with a simple cord and hair arranged in an intricate weave of braids.

"Juno," I said.

She stopped in front of me with a confused smile. "Yes, I am," she said, holding out her hand to help me to my feet. "And you are?"

I took her hand and scrambled up. Now that I was standing, I could see the water off to my right was a small river, sunlight glinting off of its roiling surface. There were a few trees on the far side, but most of the world around me was just grass.

Juno was still waiting for me to answer. "You don't recognize me?" I asked.

"Sorry, no," she said with a shake of her head. "Should I?"

"We've met," I said. "I'm Amanda Clarke. My mother was a student of your sister's."

"My sister has students?" Juno said, both amazed and amused in equal measures.

How did she not know that? "We've met face to face three times before," I said. "We've been aware of each other far more than that."

"I'm afraid I don't really know what you're talking about," she said. "I've been alone here for what I would have to say has been centuries. I stopped trying to keep track quite some time ago."

"Where are we?" I asked, looking around.

"I don't know where," she said with a careless shrug.

"I need to get back," I said. "I got yanked here mid-battle. I'm sure my friends are in danger."

"I'm so sorry, but I'm afraid that's not possible," she said.

"What do you mean?" I asked, but didn't wait for an answer. I went back into the world of threads and reached out for the time portal.

But it wasn't there.

I searched through all the threads around me looking for some way out of where I was or, failing that, some way to call for help. I was frantic and dimly aware that I wasn't paying as much attention to my physical body as I ought to be.

But if I couldn't get home again, what difference would my physical health make?

I expanded my awareness, larger and larger, but all I sensed was the most basic of living things. Grass, things that lived on grass, things that ate the things that lived on grass.

I was just turning my attention skyward when something enveloped me, surrounding me even as large as I had become, then gently pulling me back in.

I came back into my body and sucked in breath after breath. Juno was sitting in front of me much as Patricia had less than an hour before, only she had reached across to hold both of my hands.

"I had a feeling that wouldn't work," she said. "But I'm glad you tried. It answers some of my most nagging questions."

"How did I get here?" I demanded.

"I'm not quite sure," she said, getting to her feet with the ease of a dancer. Then she held out a hand once more to help me up. 'Perhaps we can figure it out together. Are you hungry? You must be after that bout of magical effort. I'm surprised you didn't damage your mind. Well, come on, then." And without waiting for an answer, she turned and started walking away.

I stood motionless for a moment, trying to recall what had happened. Something had been feeding Patricia power, and she had been doing something to disguise that fact from me. I should have felt the strangeness of it, but she had masked it as her own brand of magic quite effectively.

The moment I had realized what she was up to, she cut me off from everything. With one blow.

"Are we outside of time?" I asked as I ran to catch up with Juno.

"No, I don't believe so," she said, slowing her steps until I was walking beside her.

"But you *are* a time witch," I said.

"I was once," she said. "I can't touch time anymore. My sister took that from me when she imprisoned me here. But I can still see story."

"Miss Zenobia imprisoned you here?" I asked. "I thought she was trying to rescue you. I thought that was the whole point of maintaining the time portal."

"I don't know exactly what you're talking about," she said. "But I do know my sister always had a very different world view from me." We reached a clearing in the grass, and I saw a low sod house that looked more like what the Vikings had built than prairie settlers, more round and hut-like and less squared off like it wanted to be a log cabin. Somewhere near the top of the structure, there must have been a smoke hole because a little curl of smoke was just visible over the grassy roof whenever there was a lull in the breeze.

Juno ducked inside the open doorway, and I followed, stopping just inside to let my eyes adjust to the darkness within. There was a fire pit in the center of the space, but the smoke hole must have some sort of cover over it to keep out the rain, because very little light was filtering down from it. Juno bent over a pot that hung over the banked fire and threw in a handful of chopped green herbs from a bowl on the floor before stirring it with a long wooden spoon.

"You built all this yourself?" I asked, looking over the low bed opposite the fire from the door, the table and sturdy stool made of wood to my left, and the shelves along the wall to my right filled with all manners of things from scrolls and books to ceramic pots and wooden bowls.

"In a matter of speaking," Juno said. Then I saw she had a wand in her hand. She gave it a little flick, and one of the bowls sailed across the room to her outstretched hand.

"It must be lonely," I said.

"I keep waiting for people to arrive, but I don't think I'll live to see that happen," she said with a sad smile as she ladled steaming stew into the bowl, then set it on the table. She waved me over to sit on the stool.

"I believe we must be near the site of what will one day be the city of St. Paul," I said. "But it doesn't look right. There should be trees, for one thing. And we should be standing on a ridge overlooking the river." Juno summoned a wooden spoon over to the table, then settled herself on the end of her bed to watch me eat it.

"I'm not surprised it doesn't look right," she said as I blew on the first spoonful of stew. "There is still another ice age to go before this looks like what will exist in our time."

"How do you know that?" I asked.

"Story magic," she said. "It's not easy-to-read stories that weren't made by people, but I've had a lot of time to practice."

"You're awfully calm about all this," I said. "Aren't you trapped here?"

She shrugged again. "I was incredibly angry for the first hundred years or so. But I couldn't keep it up."

I took a bite of the stew. The meat was very lean and probably would have been tough if she hadn't been cooking it for hours. The herbs she had thrown in complemented each other well, but didn't remotely make up for the lack of salt.

Some of what I was thinking must have shown on my face because she said, "you're lucky you got here in springtime and not the dead of winter."

"I left in the middle of a blizzard," I said.

"What year?"

"I'm from 2019, but I was in 1928 when that witch Patricia cut me out of time," I said.

"That sounds horrifying," she said.

"Didn't the same happen to you?" I asked.

"No," she said. "I sort of got myself stuck here. But I was fighting with my sister at the time. She has some sneaky spells. They don't take effect right away."

"She put part of her self inside of a box to talk to my friends and I after she died," I said. "Or so we thought. It turns out she put the rest of her self somewhere else. We don't know where, or what she's waiting for."

"It sounds like she's grown in power since our fight," Juno said. "I guess I have as well, with what power I have left."

"You explained time magic to me once," I said. "And the magic of stories. You wanted to be my mentor."

"I'm afraid that wasn't me," she said. "Something else must be wearing my face."

"You look exactly the same," I said. "Not just physically. The pattern of your threads is the same."

"More than just my face then," she said, and finally something I said changed that look of Zen acceptance on her face to a slight frown.

"Do you know anything at all about the time bridge?" I asked. She shook her head. "Miss Zenobia built it. She said she did it with your help. She said the two of you reached out to each other across time to construct it. Your essence is suffused throughout the entire thing."

"How curious," she said. But I wasn't sure she believed me. I set down my spoon and shifted my awareness to the world of threads again. She sensed me looking at her in that realm and politely opened herself up to me.

I blinked back into the mundane world. "I would swear it was you. Perhaps it's some future version of you? Or maybe a you from the past that you can't remember?"

"There are no gaps in my memory," she said. "Since my sister's spell blocked me from using my time magic, all I have left is story. And I know my own story very, very well. Nothing is missing from my memory."

"I believe you," I said. "But honestly, a future you makes more sense. If you are always here, in this spot, you must exist across time all the way to my day."

She sighed. "I suppose, as my sister's protégée, you share her feelings about these sorts of things?"

"I don't think so," I said. "I mean, she died before I met her, so I'm not exactly her protégée."

"Interesting," she said. "You do know why we fought?"

"Tell me," I said.

"She thought I was meddling too much in time," Juno said. "We were guardians of a grove where the veil between worlds was thinnest, one of the rare ones where time itself was affected. I mastered time magic by studying what happened in that grove. At first, Zenobia was as interested as I was. But once I started trying to use my magic to change things, she began to disapprove. She saw it as meddling in the proper order of things."

"Was it?" I asked.

"I don't think so," she said. "Story magic has been a skill of mine since I was very young. I could see how it was inextricable from time magic, although Zenobia didn't think they were the same at all. As I said, she had a very different world view from me. I tried to explain. Reading the story of a thing or place or person, it wasn't just seeing what had happened in the past."

"You see the future?" I asked.

She gave me an indulgent smile. "Not the way charlatans claim to. It isn't like that. It comes from the story. If you know everything about how a story began, you can see how it has to end. Right?"

"I would think there was always a place for random chance," I said.

"There is," she said. "But not as much as we'd like to think. If you can read a person deeply enough, you can tell how they're going to respond to anything even before they do. And if you keep reading, you can tell how everyone else is going to respond to that. And so on."

"I guess," I said.

"I wasn't meddling with time," she said. "I was just tweaking some stories. Not many. Just ones that were barreling towards very bad ends that I didn't think deserved them. I never did anything without reading into all possible outcomes first with my story magic. I was very careful."

I think I might have flinched when she said that. I had just been thinking when she used the word "deserved" that what she was saying was starting to sound a bit like the hubris Sophie and Brianna had accused me of. And then she unwittingly threw my own words back at me.

"You said you know your own story best of all," I said.

"I do," she said, with a little smile, like she knew what I was going to say next.

"So you know that what I was theorizing—about a future you still being here in my time—isn't possible," I said.

"It's not," she said. "Shall I tell you what I've seen?"

"Sure," I said guardedly.

"I've been waiting for you," she said. "I've been waiting for such a long time. It feels like coming to the end of a very long book, and now I can close the cover."

"Your story's over?" I asked. She smiled and nodded. I swallowed hard before asking, "and mine?"

"I don't know yet," she said, still smiling. "We'll see, I guess. We'll certainly have plenty of time for me to learn your whole story backward and forward."

I swore to myself that wouldn't be true. I wouldn't sit here and accept this fate the way she did. I'd find a way out.

More than that, I'd find a way back to the very moment I had left. I had a battle to finish.

CHAPTER 20

$\mathcal{A}$s it turned out, Juno had plenty of time to learn my entire story. Bushels and bushels of time. I lost track of the days, so many in a row passed almost exactly the same as all the others.

I knew that if I ever did find a way to return, it would probably be to the same moment that I left. But in a way, that made it harder. I couldn't let go of any of my feelings. I knew Nick had been restored, but had Jackson?

What more would Patricia go on to do after eliminating me? Would I get back in time to stop her, or if not, could I undo all she did?

I remembered too many books and movies with dark alternate timelines. I doubted Patricia was a Nazi, but the idea she would create a world controlled by her coven of witches didn't seem all that unlikely.

But mostly, I missed Edward. I carried that ache around all day and struggled to sleep at night.

Juno, of course, was aware of all of this. We passed the days in meditation, she showing me all she had learned about story magic. Opening our minds to each other like that, I knew I was an open book to her. She never mentioned any of it, but I could see what she was thinking in her eyes.

She didn't say it out loud, but she was certain that my feelings would fade with time. Her anger had lasted for more than a century, she had said. My feelings might last a bit longer, but she had no doubts I would end in the same calm, Zen acceptance of our common fate.

But I was determined to prove her wrong.

At first, I spent every free moment peppering her with questions, but in the end, I had to accept that she knew nothing of Patricia, Debra and Linda. She knew nothing of anything that had happened since, even before Miss Zenobia had crossed the Atlantic. She knew nothing of the time portal or how to bring it to us in our time.

After days of meditating together, I knew she was telling me the truth. She really knew nothing about any of it.

But one other thing was true: the entity making itself look like her was the one thing that bothered her.

"You don't like the fact that something is masquerading as you," I said to her one morning after our first meditation session of the day.

"Who would?" she asked with that benign smile.

"There must be a reason it chose to look like you," I said. "Did you ever encounter anything like it?"

"No, never," she said. Then she went into her sod house to fix lunch.

I let the matter drop for a few days, but I kept mulling it over. Then, on a rainy day when we were forced to stay indoors, I brought it up again.

"If that thing never encountered you, perhaps it encountered Miss Zenobia," I said. "It might have made itself resemble you because it was trying to get to her."

"Perhaps," Juno said.

"Okay, but what sort of thing would do that? And why?" I asked.

She just shrugged.

I let it go for a few more days before bringing it up again.

"This is what I think happened," I said as the two of us sat on the bank of the river. Juno had magicked up a long net out of the end of her wand and was using it to catch a fish for dinner.

"Go on," she said. She never sounded annoyed with me for coming back to this topic, and yet she never sounded particularly interested either. But I pressed on anyway.

"You and your sister had that fight," I said. I had seen the entire thing from Juno's point of view while we had meditated together. She had been coming back from a trip in the past to correct something, and Zenobia had confronted her the moment she had appeared. The fight had been intense, involving more spells than I even knew existed. Juno had fled, at first back into the time portal as Zenobia had expected her to. But then, rather than follow its path to the point in the past they both knew well, she burst out sideways, a trick Zenobia didn't know she could even do.

But Zenobia's last spell had already been coiled up inside Juno like a snake waiting to strike. She had come here, a safe place removed in space and in time from anywhere Zenobia could look. But the moment she had appeared, the spell had finally released, destroying her access to time magic and her ability to get back home.

"Zenobia expected to be able to find you on the other end. I know she was quite distraught when she realized you weren't there. That she had lost you," I said.

"I know you believe that," Juno said diplomatically. I really couldn't blame her for not being ready to forgive her sister, so I didn't argue the point.

"She came here, to St. Paul, to try to reach you," I said. "But she never did. And yet she reached something. That entity that wears your face."

"We've searched for it," she reminded me. "There's no sign of it here in this time."

"There's no sign of the portal either," I said. "That's what I'm trying to tell you. The two are connected."

Juno was quiet, but I could tell she was giving what I said serious thought for the first time. Despite everything else I had prepared to say, I remained quiet as well.

"You said that coven you fought with served this entity," Juno said.

"After the fight with our mothers, the three ended up in 1928," I said.

"But not right away," Juno said.

"Well, it's time travel," I said. "What does 'right away' mean?"

"I know you think you're going back to the moment you left to finish your battle," Juno said. "But you still will have however many years you pass here in your memory. It will seem like an instant to the others when you return, but not for you. But I know you know there are other places a person might end up. Places without a sun and moon to track across the sky and mark time."

"You think that's what happened to Patricia and the others?" I asked. "They got caught up in a timeless place?"

"I don't know what happened to them," she said and lapsed into the sort of silence that usually meant she was done talking for the day. I was resigning myself to once again drop it when, to my surprise, she suddenly spoke again.

"I said before I never encountered an entity like what you describe," she said. "It's true; I've never come face to face with anything like that. But before my sister destroyed my magic, I moved back and forth through time a lot. And I was aware of things around me. Most of them had no more interest in me than I had in them. But sometimes it felt like being watched, but by something not remotely human."

"This thing is using your likeness so that it can appear human?" I guessed.

"From what you say, I think it tricked my sister into creating that time portal in the first place," she said. "The Zenobia I knew would never agree to such a thing, and especially not if I was the one asking. She hated time magic. This entity must have been very persuasive indeed."

"So it tricked her into creating the time portal, but it didn't have control of it," I said.

"No, my sister would never allow that," Juno said. "She's always so careful, layering spells for every contingency. Nothing is ever left out of her control. You told me the portal was unstable, and when it was stable, it was locked down on both ends and guarded over by first my sister and then by you. That sounds like Zenobia's style."

"And the entity didn't like that," I said.

"I guess not," she said. "But if it did cause the rift between your mother and Patricia like you seem to believe, what was its purpose?"

"To get control of the time portal?" I said. "To take it from Miss Zenobia?"

"Then it failed," Juno said.

"It failed that time," I said, but then gasped aloud as a horrid thought dawned on me. "It failed, until I came along. How could I have been so stupid?"

"What?" Juno asked, alarmed as I pounded my fists against the ground.

"Don't you see?" I asked. "I turned down every advance it made for the two of us to work together. I never trusted it. But it was manipulating me the entire time, and I never even knew it."

"Manipulating you into doing what?" Juno asked.

"During that first fight with Patricia, I collapsed the portal down to a wormhole only I could see. So instead of three witches guarding the portal, now there was only one. Me. Then all it had to do was eliminate me. Boom. And I made it so easy." I wanted to tear my hair out.

"Wait a minute," she said. "You told me that before she turned on you, you and Patricia had restored the time bridge. Surely, once that was done, your friends will be able to see it like before."

"Maybe, but it's still too late," I said. "That wasn't the last thing we did together. The last thing we did was supposed to be creating a side bridge to take Patricia and her friends back to 1968. But that isn't what happened. When her magic flowed through me, I ended up creating scores of side bridges, reaching out to all sorts of times."

"I agree, lots of opportunities for mischief there," Juno said.

"I have to get back," I said, getting to my feet. As if I could simply walk home. "I have to stop them."

"How are you going to do that?" she asked.

I started to pace up and down the riverbank, hands curling into fists, but my brain was moving even more furiously than my body.

Then a sudden thought stopped me cold. I spun around to point a finger at Juno like I was pinning her to the spot. "Miss Zenobia removed your access to time magic."

"And I wasn't lying," Juno said warily. "I can't help you escape from here."

"That's not what I mean," I said and resumed pacing, but this time my eyes were on her instead of on the ground in front of me. "If she did it to you, then it's a thing that can be done again."

"I don't know how she did it," Juno said.

"But it can be done," I said.

"Theoretically," Juno said, a word she had picked up from me. "But what good is theory? We're still stuck here."

"It takes two witches to work across time," I said. "One on each end."

"So even if I had access to my time magic, I couldn't help you," Juno said. "And Patricia certainly won't. Or the entity she serves, although it sounds to me like that thing is using the rest of you specifically because it doesn't have time magic of its own."

"Good point," I said. I hadn't thought of that, and for a moment, that fact cooled my blood. "All the more reason for me to get back and end things before it gets what it wants."

"Were you going to tell me how you plan to do that?" Juno asked.

"That's where you come in," I said.

"I've already explained—" she started, but I cut her off.

"I'm not talking about your time magic," I said. "I'm talking about your sister."

"My sister?" Juno said.

"If you're right and this entity has no time magic, then when it pretended to be you and called out to your sister to reach across time, it convinced her—"

But this time, she interrupted me. "She did all the work herself." Then she looked up at me wonderingly. "Do you really think that's what happened?"

"Miss Zenobia is widely regarded as the most powerful witch of this age," I said.

"But she hates time magic," Juno said.

"She did," I said, "when you knew her. Centuries ago. I swear to you, her desire to reach you and make amends was real. She devoted her entire life to it. Her life, and all of her power. Given that, what *couldn't* she do?"

"You might be right," she said. "I don't want to believe it, but you might be right."

"And remember, she didn't die," I said. I sat down on the ground beside her again so our eyes would be at the same level. "She did as much as she could for the portal, left it in our charge, and put the rest of her self away. I couldn't figure out what she was waiting for, but I think I know now."

"For me," Juno said. "You think she was waiting for me."

"I think she figured out the other you was false," I said. "She didn't have enough energy left to start the search for you again. But she took what she had left and stored it until the moment that *you* found *her*."

"But how do I find her?" Juno asked. "You said you had no idea where she was."

"I still don't," I said. "But I think if you call out to her, sister to sister, she'll hear. And if you call, she'll come running."

CHAPTER 21

Doing magic with Juno was very different from doing magic with Brianna and Sophie, and not just because there were only two of us. If anything, a circle with the two of us passing power back and forth to each other was easier than doing it with three people. And our way of perceiving and working with magic was very similar. The two of us just understood each other.

But it felt like something was missing. With Brianna and Sophie, we had to work around three very different ways of seeing the world. It was tricky, but in the end, I think we had more power because of it.

On the other hand, Juno and I might be capable of the same sort of magic and so had less range, but the two of us working that magic together more than doubled our amplification.

At first, we just opened ourselves up to each other and shared our memories of Zenobia. They didn't quite match. I guess she must have changed a lot from the time in her youth with Juno had known her to when I had met a ghostly version of her centuries later. But we worked patiently, me following Juno's lead, to pick out the threads of the story and connect hers to mine.

We weren't creating a hologram version of her like I had done with Brianna and Sophie using the words of her journal. But I could sense something beginning to coalesce between us. As we teased out more and more of the story of her life through the threads before us, she took on more and more form.

It was tiring work and required a lot of focus, not just on what I was doing with Miss Zenobia's story, but also on keeping track of my physical body. My only real perception of time was when I would touch one of my body's threads and got a sense of cold that must have meant it was nearly nightfall, and later still of hunger.

At last, Juno pushed a thought towards me that we had done as much as we could. I let go of the story threads I was still holding and felt a sudden longing to go back into my physical body, but the real work was yet to begin.

Juno focused all her mind on the form between us, a collection of threads that to my perception exactly replicated what I saw when I looked at not just a person, but a witch. And a powerful witch at that. She wasn't there physically, and if my body opened its eyes, it would see nothing there but Juno still in a trance. But for all magical purposes, a witch was there.

I felt Juno call out to her sister, not so much in words, which didn't exist where we were, but just raw feelings. All her feelings: longing for reunion but also a lingering sense of betrayal, centuries of loneliness, a desire to help me with my quest.

Her calling went on and on, but no answer came back.

I felt Juno give up, and the moment she did, we were both kicked out of the magical sphere, back into our cold, cramped bodies covered in dew out in the grassy field.

I saw Juno's face crumpling in despair. I reached forward to catch her hands, but something was between us now. My hands actually started to pass through it before I snatched them back.

It hadn't felt like anything, but it looked so real.

It was the hem of a long gray dress. And I could see boots beneath it, black boots with pointed toes and buttons up the sides past the ankle.

Slowly, I looked up into the familiar face of Miss Zenobia. Steel gray hair pulled back in a severe bun to match the dour, heavy Victorian dress so out of place here on the prairie.

But her eyes were twinkling at me.

"Miss Zenobia?" I asked, no more than a whisper. The field around us was loud with insects and frogs singing at the coming of dawn. That rattling chorus must have drowned out my words. But she smiled down at me.

"Well done," she said. "I put a lot of work into you. I'm glad you didn't disappoint me."

"Um, thanks?" I said, but her attention was now on Juno.

"Juno," she said, almost coldly.

"Sister," Juno said, and her voice was downright icy.

"Please don't start fighting," I said, pressing a hand over my eyes. I needed a twenty-hour nap, at least.

"Come, Miss Amanda," Miss Zenobia said in her most schoolmarmy voice. "You summoned me here so I could end this."

"I summoned you here so you could rescue us," I said.

"Us?" Miss Zenobia said. "Do you know what she's done?"

"You don't know what she's done," I said. "Which is nothing." Ugh. I could tell by the look on her face that, despite being a teacher of charm and of magic, the grammar of that sentence was nearly physically hurting her. "You haven't actually seen your sister since the two of you fought back in the United Kingdom. What you saw after you got to St. Paul was never her."

"What do you mean?" Miss Zenobia asked.

"Something was pretending to be me," Juno said. "To trick you into doing time magic. Which I didn't even know you could do, frankly."

Miss Zenobia frowned, but didn't argue.

"If you think about it, I think you'll find it makes sense," I said. "You created a portal through time to bring Juno back to you, only she refused to go. Why would she do that?"

"Why *would* you do that?" Miss Zenobia asked her sister.

"It wasn't me," Juno said.

"Then the thing pretending to be Juno tried to get control of the portal from you," I said. "I don't know if luring your students into a battle over it was its first attempt. Maybe there were others. It doesn't matter, because it looks like it's about to succeed. You have to get me back to 1928 so I can stop it."

"I knew something was wrong," Miss Zenobia said, mostly to herself. "I could never figure out just what it was. But some things I knew."

"Is this a good time for you to explain what you meant about putting work into me?" I asked. "Since you were dead before we met, I'm having a little difficulty figuring that bit out."

"I needed a time witch," she said. "Your mother and Patricia had some skill, but I needed more than that. I needed more raw power."

"How did you get that?" I asked. Part of me really didn't want to hear the answer.

"There are spells to influence the development of a child," she said with an offhanded wave.

Yep, I was right. I really didn't want to know.

"And I'm the problem for meddling in the past," Juno grumbled. "You've changed."

"I've had to," Miss Zenobia said. "I wouldn't have done it if it hadn't been extremely necessary. I knew I wouldn't live long enough to do what needed to be done. I had to plan for a future I knew I'd never see without very strong magic." Then she was smiling at me again. "But thanks to you, I *am* seeing it."

I pressed my thumb and fingertips to the bridge of my nose and took deep breaths to calm my anger. I hated the idea that I had been shaped since before birth to serve some small function for a witch older than time.

The word hubris leaped to mind again. Just wait until I told Sophie about Miss Zenobia and the long game she had been playing.

When at last I was pretty sure I could keep my calm, I looked up at the sisters again. "I need to get back to where I was before Patricia cut me out of time. Can you do it?"

"I'm not physically here," Miss Zenobia said.

"Great," I grumbled. "That's just great. What good is your ghost form exactly?"

"It's completely worthless," Miss Zenobia said, and I could tell my annoyed tone was angering her.

"Her physical form is still in your time. 2019," Juno said to me. "Zenobia can open a portal to that time, and you and Patricia just created a bridge from there to 1928."

"Okay," I said. "Good."

"But I'm not meant to go," Juno said, and that air of Zen acceptance was all over her again.

"No, I don't think you are," Miss Zenobia said disdainfully.

"Would you two stop it?" I snapped.

"I came here to end her, not to rescue her," Miss Zenobia said.

"Then why did you leave your body behind?" I asked.

"That was the nature of the summoning *you* performed," she said.

"I've been over and over my story," Juno said, although which of the two of us she was talking to, I didn't know for sure. "But the threads of my past and present can't point me to what happens at the end."

"That's because what's about to happen isn't part of your past and present," I said. "It's part of mine."

Juno's eyes widened. "That could be true. I saw you coming. I waited for you. And I always knew I'd see my sister one last time. But everything else has always been a blank for me."

"All my plans were for the purpose of removing you from every timeline. For good," Miss Zenobia said stubbornly.

"Not exactly," I said. "I know part of you is still angry about whatever happened between you when you were young. But if you think about it objectively, I think you'll find that what you really feel like has to be removed from all time isn't your sister. It's the entity that pretended to be your sister. The entity that really wants an all-access pass to unlimited time travel. Which it's going to get if you don't get me home to stop it."

A calmness passed over Miss Zenobia's face as she closed her eyes. It had a forced quality at first, but as she ruminated, it became more genuine. Her anger was gone. Or at least damped down for now.

At last, she opened her eyes and looked at me.

"Juno and I can get you home," she said. "That's simple enough. It will be a onetime bridge through time, and I'll be destroying it behind you the entire way. It might be a rough ride."

"I can handle it," I said.

"I know you can," she said. "But it's going to be the end of me. I saved as much of my self and my power as I could, but that will take all I have left."

"I'll help," Juno said. "As much as I can."

"You won't live much longer, you know," Miss Zenobia said. "The end of a witch's lifespan is flexible, but not that flexible."

"I've been here long enough," Juno said. "It's time to move on. To the next world, whatever that might be."

Miss Zenobia reached a hand down towards her sister, and Juno reached up as if to take it, but their fingers passed through each other.

"As I said, getting you home is the easy part," Miss Zenobia said, turning her attention back to me. "But what do you intend to do next?"

"Well," I said. "You took away Juno's access to time magic, right? I need you to teach me that spell."

CHAPTER 22

Iss Zenobia wasn't wrong. The spell to bring me back across time appeared incredibly simple for her. I barely had time to shift my awareness to the world of threads before I was hurtling down a long tunnel from the very distant past towards the last place I had been standing in time.

It wasn't as narrow as the wormhole, and yet I was moving through it so quickly I couldn't sense anything outside of it. I did feel the way it kept collapsing behind me. If I slowed down even for a second, I would be caught up in that destruction. I would be lost.

But I wasn't the one in control of how fast I was moving. That was Miss Zenobia. At first, it was like she was holding my hand, and Juno was holding my other. But the further along the tunnel we traveled, the more Zenobia started to fade away.

And then I was back. I was outside both my real and magical selves for the moment. I was at the anchor point of the bridge in 2019. I could see my magical form collapsing on itself in the middle of the time bridge, Patricia's magical form towering over it. And I could see my physical body still sitting cross-legged in the backyard in 1928.

It looked perfectly normal: still alive, still breathing. Despite the fact I had been using a physical body in the grassy fields before the last ice age, I don't think it had left this place for more than a microsecond. I don't know how that worked.

But what I was mostly aware of was my magical form. Patricia had just cut all the threads attaching it to the world in one swift blow. She was still there, standing over it, her own threads glowing with a sinister light. I could tell she was gloating.

That changed as I hurled myself from the anchor point in 2019 back into my magical form. And Juno was still there with me. She was more a diaphanous cloud than a human-like form, but I felt her all around me. I don't know if Patricia could sense her presence, but she definitely saw the results when Juno reformed all those threads at once.

There is no sound in the world of threads, but I supposed inside her own head, Patricia was shrieking with rage. I was subverting her triumphant moment. I felt a little smug about that.

Then I felt her gathering energy. Juno wrapped herself around me, much as she had that first time I had met her when she kept me from dissipating my consciousness into nothingness trying to find the portal that wasn't there. Now she was acting as my shield. With her there protecting me, I didn't have to prepare my own defenses right away. I could spare the time to figure out where Patricia was drawing that power from.

And there it was. The entity. How had I missed seeing it before? It stood outside of time, not on the time bridge, but the dark power it was flowing into Patricia had a magnitude like Niagara Falls. Even now, it was still pouring into her.

But for now, I ignored that. I turned my attention to the bridge itself. While Juno protected me from Patricia's darkness-infused attacks, I made quick work of undoing all we had done before. Within the blink of an eye, the time portal was once more the size of a worm-hole, imperceptible to all but the most powerful of time witches. There was only a slight bulging in the middle where Patricia and I still stood. But having nothing left to support it, that too was on the brink of collapse. Patricia, intent on attacking me, didn't even notice how precarious our position had become.

But the entity, still floating just outside of time and the portal itself, did.

This time, when the creature shrieked in pain and rage, it sounded nothing like Juno. Its cries were not remotely human. And being in the world of threads, it wasn't a sound, anyway; it was an assault on my mind. And my mind was repelled by it with such intensity I nearly retreated to my physical body.

Then I felt Juno, still protecting me but also supporting me. She guided my awareness to my other supports, Brianna in the present and Sophie in the past. I still had their strength and stability to draw from.

As hard as it was to do, I tuned out the superhuman entity shrieking in my mind and focused only on Patricia. With the spell Miss Zenobia had taught me, I cut her off first from the entity and its firehose of power, and then from her own time magic.

She winked out of the world of threads, and I turned my attention to 1928 to see her body slump to the ground. Debra and Linda rushed to her sides, but I could see she was still alive.

Alive, and possibly someday still a threat. I pulled what had to be a painful amount of power out of Sophie and Brianna, but I needed it all to do what had to be done.

Miss Zenobia had taught me the spell to cut away time magic, but Juno had taught me a thing, too. She had taught me how to do her sideways trick, to end up in some other time and space than the portal led to.

I took hold of those three and flung them through time. I was aiming for 1968—it was probable that they weren't bad witches outside of bad influences, and even Miss Zenobia herself had been seduced by that dark entity—but I don't know if I hit it. I'm not even sure if they all landed together.

I shifted my awareness into 1928 and looked towards the tower. Without Linda to power the glamour, it couldn't stand. It looked like it was melting back into the bedrock. The other witches were there, save the one in Wisconsin. Most of them didn't have anything like the power Patricia, Linda and Debra had had, but I didn't want to take any chances. I caught them up too and scattered them throughout time, as far back into time as I could throw them. The one in Wisconsin might still be a threat, but she would have to find a way to act alone. I wasn't worried about her.

The entity was not happy about this course of events. It rushed at me, gnashing to get within the portal. But it no longer existed within the fabric of what was now the size of a wormhole. The parts I had cut away to reduce its size had been the entity-infused parts.

All that was left were the smaller components created from Miss Zenobia's own self.

I could feel her within it, in the invisible walls that were close all around me. Then Juno, or the tattered remains of what had once been Juno, fell away from me. She no longer had the strength to shield me, but the time for that had passed. I sent her all my love and gratitude as she, too, settled into the walls of the portal itself.

The thing Miss Zenobia had intended to build with the help of her long-lost sister now, finally, contained them both. And the two of them together stood strong against the entity. But their time was at an end.

And it was up to me to end it.

The entity desperately wanted my attention. I knew the moment I regarded it in any way it would change form. It had become Juno to tempt Miss Zenobia, and that had worked on her, but not on me. What would it do to reach me? What form would it take?

My mother?

I would do just about anything for a single five-minute conversation with my mother.

But I was never going to get it. My mother was dead and gone, and she had taken her whole life's story with her. I couldn't change that.

But there were still a couple of things I could change.

I turned my attention to the threads and made sure, one last time, that Nick was okay. I found him still standing beside Brianna in the backyard of the school in 2019. He was worried about me. I wished, again, for just a moment to say goodbye to him.

But it wasn't to be. The time portal had to come down, now. And I had to be on the other side of it.

I reached out for Sophie, sending her a mental reassurance before I streamed her through the fading wormhole. She hadn't enjoyed that trip the last three times; she really didn't enjoy it this time.

But she was safe in 2019 now, with Brianna and Nick.

Nick, who still didn't remember Jackson. There was definitely one last thing I had to fix before the time portal collapsed for good.

I focused on the threads emanating from the rabbit. They were dwindling away, the throbs of their dying light matching the fading of the time portal.

When the time portal went down, all hope of recovering Jackson was going to go down with it.

But why?

I moved closer to 2019 to get a better look. As I drew nearer, the threads grew stronger. I could sense his presence, not quite in the world yet, but nearly so. How was I doing that?

I tried feeding my power into the threads, but despite how they glowed with my magic in them, the moment I moved back towards 1928, they immediately started dying again.

There was only one answer. I was the problem.

Was the entity somehow responsible for this? Was Jackson leverage to keep me where the entity wanted me?

The entity was still yowling in rage then pleading in a wordless rush of promises I was tuning out, not easy to do when all of that was happening as an assault on my mind. But even without looking directly at the entity, I could see none of the threads lead to it.

No, only my actions were affecting it.

I went back to the 2019 end of the portal and tried again to fill the threads with power, all the power I could spare. I was really going to pay for this later. But again, when I moved to 1928, they immediately started to die.

I couldn't go back to 1928. I couldn't be with Edward.

I couldn't even say goodbye.

I was aware of him watching for me, Otto by his side. I moved my magical form as close to him as I could, but I couldn't leave the time portal. I knew the moment I did it would collapse, and Jackson would be gone for good.

I think he could sense me there, though. He was reaching out a hand towards me, anguish in his eyes but also something like acceptance. Otto was saying something to him I couldn't hear. I don't think Edward was hearing him either. His attention was all on me, or what he could perceive of me.

In that moment, I knew he would be safe. My wards and Otto's boys would protect him. I just knew it. He was going to have a long life.

Without me.

I could feel the last of the time portal collapsing around me like a black hole. I had to get out of there. As much as I would have preferred to just fade away in that moment with Zenobia and Juno, I had to live. For Jackson's sake.

With the entity's cries still in my mind, I hurled myself out of the time portal, back into 2019.

"Amanda!" Nick cried, but Sophie and Brianna held him back. They knew I still had work to do.

And I was weeping as I did it, but it was the only way to keep the entity from ever gaining control over it.

I destroyed the last vestiges of the time portal, no larger than a thread now. The thing that was our sacred duty, that we three had been called to protect, was no more.

And I no longer had any way to get back to Edward.

I fell to my knees when I knew it was done, pressing the heels of my hands into my eyes as if that could stop the tears.

"Is it done?" Nick asked. He had fallen to his knees beside me and put an arm around me to support me, but he was looking up at Sophie and Brianna as he asked that question.

"I feel like it is," Brianna said, but she sounded uncertain.

"Do you remember the boy, Jackson Smith?" Sophie asked.

"Brianna asked me that before," he said. "What does that mean? Who is he? Why should I remember him?"

I sunk lower until my forehead was pressed to the cold earth of the orchard. Had I just given up Edward for nothing?

"Amanda?" Sophie asked, touching the hair on the back of my neck gently.

"I don't understand," I said. "I did everything. Everything! Why isn't he here?"

No one spoke, but Nick kept his arm around me as I sobbed.

"If you did everything you could, then this couldn't be because of you," Brianna said. "Logically, it just can't."

"No, it was me," I said and forced my emotions back under control. "It *was* me. I know that much is true. I thought it was because I had wanted to stay in 1928. But I didn't do it. I came here instead. And the time portal has been destroyed completely. No one can use it now, not even me."

"I don't know much about time magic," Brianna said. "But maybe I can change that. The library I found in Boston, it has all sorts of volumes of magic lore that were believed lost. And more that no one ever knew even existed. There must be an answer in there somewhere. I won't rest until I find it."

"I think it's too late," I said. "I think he really is gone."

I sat up and put my hands in my pockets. For a moment I thought the rabbit had gone, but it was still there, just buried deep.

I held it in my hands for a moment. Then, despite my exhaustion, I forced myself into the world of threads to look at it.

It looked just as it had the last time I had looked at it in 2019. Completely inert. Not connected to anything, not even to me.

I came back into the world to find Sophie and Brianna sitting so that the three of us formed a circle.

"What do we have to do?" Sophie asked.

"There's nothing we *can* do," I said. "This rabbit, it has a connection in 1928 to Edward and to Ivy. Or her house, anyway, since she's dead. I saw that before, but I didn't tell you. I guess my being in the past disrupted the series of events that were supposed to end in this boy, Jackson. But it's too late to fix it now."

"But that doesn't make sense," Brianna said. "Ivy died months ago.

The boy only disappeared when Sophie and I were away. So what changed then?"

"You did," Sophie said, looking at me. "That's when you started seeing Edward, like, all the time."

"But I can't anymore," I said. "The time portal is gone. There's not a hint of it left that anyone can use. I'll never see Edward again. So why isn't the boy back?"

They each took one of my hands, not to work magic together but just to lend me a very mundane but necessary sort of strength.

We sat like that for a long time, not speaking. My stomach rumbled, and I realized that, with all the many months I had spent alone with Juno before the last ice age, the most recent memories in my mind, I had no idea when I had last eaten in 2019.

And just like that, thinking of Juno, I knew what I had to do.

As I raised my wand, Sophie and Brianna both lunged toward me, crying out in alarm, but they weren't fast enough.

With one fell swoop, I sliced through my own magical self.

I cut off my own access to time magic.

The world around me was shattering, and my magical senses were burning with sudden blindness. I wanted to lie down and die.

But instead, I looked to Nick. And I could see it in his eyes. He remembered the boy. His face started to split into a huge grin, and his arms started to wrap around me in a bear hug of gratitude.

But I couldn't hold on to the world anymore. The pain was too much. I barely felt my nose hitting the dirt as I face-planted to the ground.

Then everything was blessed darkness.

CHAPTER 23

$\mathcal{I}$ had spent the first twenty years of my life not knowing that magic was real. As I look back, that's kind of ironic. I mean, without that magical compulsion keeping me in my hometown until Cynthia came for me, my life would have been very different.

But it hadn't been a bad life, as I kept reminding myself about a hundred times a day now. I had had an apartment I was just barely affording, but I had never actually missed making rent. The Schneidermans had been constantly pushing food on me, so I never had worries there. And the local library might have been small, but I had been intimate with the mechanics of interlibrary loan by the time I was twelve.

If it hadn't been a particularly happy life, it hadn't been particularly unhappy either.

I couldn't say the same of life after I found out magic was real. "Unhappy" didn't begin to scratch the surface of what I was feeling lately.

But even hurt as I was—physically, emotionally, but most of all magically—I wouldn't trade the last few months for anything.

And it wasn't like I'd lost all my magic. I could no longer see the world of threads, not even to the level that Juno had been able to back before the ice age. I guess I had cut myself more deeply than Miss Zenobia had done to her sister. So time travel was totally out of the question. Reading the stories of things in the threads that defined their existence was no longer possible, either. But my bond with my wand was as strong as ever.

I could, for instance, use it as Juno had to move things around the kitchen. I could make everything dance like objects in a Disney film: cups and saucers landing with a happy clatter on a tray as the kettle that wasn't even plugged in heated itself up to boiling and the tea arced through the air in a spray of leaves from the storage canister to the open teapot.

Once I had magicked several slices of bread into and out of the toaster and summoned butter and marmalade from the refrigerator, I put my wand away to carry the tray up to the library with my own two hands.

"Knock, knock," I said as I came into the library. Three kittens raced across the carpet to lunge at my shoelaces, necessitating a complete stop to prevent being tripped up.

"Oh, tea," Brianna said, her head popping up from behind a stack of books so tall it looked like she had been building a fort out of them. She got up and ran to take the tray from me, making tisking sounds at the kittens now tumbling and rolling over each other at my feet.

"And toast," I said. "Which is in no way a bribe or meant to put pressure on you in any way."

"Of course it isn't," Brianna said, finding an open corner of the table where the tray could just fit. "But it wouldn't be necessary, anyway. I nearly have it all put together. I'm just checking a last few things. How are you doing?"

Then she looked me right in the face, a decidedly un-Brianna thing for her to do. Sophie was the usual one for those long assessing gazes.

The corners of her mouth went down, and I knew she could tell I had been crying, just like I had been daily since I had cut myself off from Edward, time, and magic all in one day.

"I'm okay," I said. Her eyes kept searching my face, as if she didn't quite believe me. "Really," I said more emphatically.

Brianna summoned a smile, then let her gaze wander over to the mountains of books. "You've been doing other magic?"

"Nothing serious. Just amusing myself," I said.

"That's good," she said, nodding a bit too enthusiastically.

"Well, it's like you said. I cut myself off from a power most witches never even have, but what I have left is perfectly adequate to be an ordinary witch," I said.

"That's not exactly what I said," she said, frowning at my attempt at humor.

"More or less," I said. "Where's Sophie? I made enough for everyone. I thought we could sit together for a bit."

"Oh," Brianna said, just noticing the size of the tray I had handed to her. "I believe she's outside in the garden. Nice day and all."

"I'll go get her, then," I said. "Don't start without us."

But she was already in her chair, back behind the book fort, lost within numerous texts that I was half-convinced she was reading all at once.

I found Sophie in the orchard. She wasn't meditating or dancing; she was just strolling around and looking at the trees themselves. The weather had finally made a turn for the warmer, and buds were just beginning to appear on the tips of the branches.

"Hey, Sophie," I said.

"Hey, Amanda," she said.

Then I noticed her clothes. The shiny red jacket and the matching hat set at a jaunty angle over her perfect hair. Those were her traveling clothes.

"Where are you going?" I asked.

"Back to New Orleans," she said. "I was just about to go up and tell you."

"What, five minutes before you headed out the door?" I asked.

"I have a couple of hours before Mr. Trevor drives me to the airport," she said. Then, in a softer voice, "don't be mad."

"Is that why you're sneaking away? Because you're afraid I'm going to be mad?" I asked. As if I could hurt anyone now, me with my dancing Disney kitchen skills.

"I'm not sneaking," Sophie said. "And I didn't want to upset you, but I guess I have, anyway. That wasn't my intention."

"Why are you going back to New Orleans?" I asked.

"Actually, I'm meeting with the private investigator Nick hired," she said, lifting her chin. "Even after everything that's happened, we still don't know what happened to our mothers."

"Brianna is still sure her mother just died of natural causes," I said.

"Maybe yours did too," Sophie said. "It certainly seems that way. And maybe my mother was just in the wrong place at the wrong time when she died."

"If you believe that, why go?" I asked.

"I'm not trying to get revenge or anything. I'm not even trying to find out how she died. As I said, I guess we know all that. But something happened to all of them. Between the memory of Patricia's amulet and the photos in the newspaper until the point where our memories begin, there's a lot of unexplored territory."

"I guess it *is* what you came here to find out in the first place," I said. "Will you be coming back?"

"Of course," Sophie said, but her eyes refused to meet mine.

"Yeah," I said, kicking the dusty ground. "I guess there's no reason for you to. With the time portal gone, so is our calling."

"That's not the only thing holding us together," Sophie said. "Not anymore."

"No?" I said. "Because I'm pretty sure that Brianna is just wrapping up whatever she's working on now, and then she's heading back to Boston."

"Did she say that?" Sophie asked.

"No, but I can feel it," I said.

"Well, what about you?" she asked. "Are you going back to your hometown?"

"No," I said. "There's nothing for me there. Not anymore." I kicked the ground again. "Not that there's anything for more me here, either." Sophie opened her mouth to say something, but I was already hating myself for how maudlin I was sounding. "Come on," I said, forcing a little cheer. "I made tea for all of us. It's up in the library. You said you had a couple of hours?"

"Tea sounds great," Sophie said and followed me back into the house and up to the library.

Brianna had moved several stacks of books, leaving half of the table bare so she could set out the tea things in front of three of the chairs. She looked up as we came in, but the expression on her face was grim.

"What is it?" I asked. What could have possibly happened in the handful of minutes I had been outside?

"Sit down," she said, pulling out a chair for me. I did, but only because it seemed like the fastest way to get her talking. "What's happening with Jackson Smith?"

Of all the things I had been expecting her to say, that hadn't been it. It was so disorienting it took me a moment to even recognize the name.

"Jackson Smith?" I said. "The last time I talked to Nick, he was still in foster care. Nick was trying to help him find a more permanent situation, but he said it might not be easy. He's a withdrawn, moody kid. That and his age are against him finding adoptive parents. Which is a shame; Nick says the kid has real talent. He has a unique way of observing the world, apparently."

"So you haven't met him?" Brianna asked.

"No, I never have," I said. "Why do you ask?"

"Because I know who he is," she said.

"You don't look happy about it," I said.

"It's not that," she said. "It all makes sense now; that gives me a feeling of everything being right with the world. I'm just not sure I should tell you."

"I think you've come too far not to now," Sophie said.

Brianna looked up at her, but whatever she had been about to say evaporated as she noticed Sophie's clothes. "You're leaving?"

"So are you," Sophie shot back.

"I was going to say something before I left," Brianna said.

"I'm not mad," I said. "I know you both have things calling you home. Sophie has the mystery of her lifetime to solve, and I can see how being away from your other library is causing you nearly physical pain, Brianna."

"You can?" Brianna asked.

"It's kind of obvious," Sophie said, picking up one of the books to glance at the spine. "Even if you have your friends from Boston sending you everything you want, it just isn't the same."

"No, it isn't," Brianna said.

"You were working on things too," I said. "Your research. Before we were all called here. Now you can get back to it."

"But what will you do?" Brianna asked.

"Stay here with Mr. Trevor, I guess," I said. "Not that there's anything that needs doing here anymore."

"It could still be a school," Brianna said, a touch too eagerly.

"I barely know any magic," I said. "There's no way I could teach it."

"Don't sell yourself short," Sophie said. "And anyway, I think I can see what Brianna is aiming at."

"You can?" Brianna asked.

"Sure," Sophie said. "You think this would be the perfect school for orphaned, withdrawn, moody kids with real talent and unique ways of seeing the world."

"We're going to need a new plaque," I said. "A much bigger plaque, if that's what we're going with."

"But don't you think it's a good idea?" Brianna asked.

"I would do anything for this kid," I said, annoyed at how my voice choked up again. "I think I've made that really clear. But I'm pretty sure schools need qualifications and certifications and all sorts of things a twenty-something ex-waitress doesn't have. And I don't even know how a school adopts a kid."

"It wouldn't be just you," Sophie said. "Mr. Trevor will still be here with you. And there's more than enough money in the trust fund to hire a lawyer to sort the rest of it out for you."

"I don't know," I said. "That sounds really huge."

"You could help kids like Jackson, and if you happened to find a few young witches in need of a little training, well, bonus," Sophie said. "It just feels like one of us should pick up where Miss Zenobia left off. She did more than guard a time portal, after all."

"I don't think I'm the best choice to take over for Miss Zenobia," I said. "And besides, she had more than a century under her belt before she decided to open a school."

"But you'll think about it?" Brianna asked.

"Sure," I said. "I'll think about it. Now tell me what you don't want to tell me."

She bit down hard on her lip and seemed to still be considering not speaking, but in the end she gave a quick nod of her head and pushed some books aside to pull out a stack of computer printouts.

"Jackson Smith," she said, putting down a copy of the police report from the car accident. "Nick is correct that he has no living relatives, at least not any closer than a sixth or seventh cousin." She slapped down the next piece of paper, another page from the same report, this one a photo taken by the coroner. "His father's name was Hugh Smith. I traced his family line all the way back to England in the 1600s, but it's not relevant."

"Way to be thorough," Sophie said appreciatively as she spread butter on a square of cold toast.

"Can we skip ahead to the relevant part?" I asked.

Brianna looked actually pained, but Sophie gave her a little nod of encouragement. "All right," she said, shuffling through her papers. "His mother, of course, also has no living relatives. She was an only child of an only child. But if you track that family stick back to the 1930s, you get to here."

She found the page she wanted and frowned at it for a moment before setting it down on the table between Sophie and me.

"Wow," I said, looking at the black-and-white photo of a girl of about eight. "She sure has Jackson's eyes. Or the other way around, I guess."

"Yes," Brianna said, but something in the way she was fidgeting in her chair told me to look again.

The girl was familiar, but I couldn't place her. "This was taken in the 30s?"

"No, in 1956," Brianna said.

"Come on, look at her clothes," Sophie said with something like her customary teasing back in her voice for the first time since I had destroyed the time portal.

"I don't know how I could know her, then," I said. "Who is she?"

"Her name is Amanda," Brianna said, and I lunged towards the picture again. But it didn't look remotely like me. Not with that straight brown hair and those dark eyes. "Amanda McTavet-Scott."

"Edward had a daughter?" Sophie asked.

"But why does she look like..." I trailed off, not sure I even knew what I was seeing. The hair was like his. The color of the eyes was like his. But the mischief in those eyes, the bright color in those apple cheeks? She hadn't gotten that from Edward. No, those reminded me of... "Coco?"

Brianna smiled softly. "Exactly. Coco."

And then I put it all together. I slumped back in my chair, hands over my eyes. "Coco. Of course. Not Ivy. This had nothing to do with Ivy at all."

"This girl was born in 1948?" Sophie said, and I dropped my hands from my eyes to see Brianna nod that she was correct. "So if you had stayed with Edward..."

"No Jackson," I said. "No Amanda McTavet-Scott. No one in between either."

"1948," Sophie said. "That's a long time after 1928."

"Yes," Brianna said. She glanced up at me as if gaging whether I was ready to hear the rest. I gave a little nod. "Coco had a bit of an adventuresome youth. I've tracked it through secondary sources, but I really hope she left diaries behind somewhere because I'm sure that they would be just fabulous. So, wild youth. But then, to everyone's surprise, she abruptly settled down and got married in 1941. But not to Edward; not at first. Her first husband was still in law school when they married, but had a bright future in front of him, by all accounts. She loved this fellow madly. Unfortunately, just a few months into their marriage, Pearl Harbor happened. He enlisted, was sent to the Pacific, and never came home."

"Killed?" I asked.

"Worse, missing in action," Brianna said. "His remains were recovered from an unnamed island in the Pacific, but not until long after Coco died of old age. She spent the rest of her life never knowing where he was or if he was ever coming home to her."

"Poor Coco," Sophie said. "Such a cruel fate for such a vivacious girl."

"I guess that explains it," I said, not looking at either of them. "Edward must have felt much the same. Not knowing if he was waiting in vain or not."

"He was a bachelor when they married in 1948," Brianna said. "Six months before Amanda was born."

"Amanda," Sophie said. "I guess they were both still thinking of you."

I nodded, but I didn't trust myself to form words.

"But one thing I still don't understand," Sophie said. "Why wasn't it enough when Amanda came back to 2019 and destroyed the time portal? Why wasn't that enough to bring Jackson back?"

"Because," I said before Brianna could speak, "I had sworn to Edward that nothing would keep us apart. And as long as I had time magic, I would never stop trying to find a way back to him."

But now I had to. I hadn't realized until just that minute that part of me was still plotting a way to get back to him. Other wardrobes, other time portals, other magic.

But I had to stop with those plans now, no matter how idle I told myself that thinking was.

I had to let him go.

But at least I still had a piece of him I could look after.

"I'll do it," I said. "The school thing. Mr. Trevor and I will figure out a way. Jackson isn't going to get lost in the system. Not if I can save him."

CHAPTER 24

$\mathcal{A}$s it turned out, the hardest part about turning Miss Zenobia Weekes' School for Exceptional Young Ladies into the McTavet-Scott Academy for Exceptional Youngsters wasn't the legal stuff. Mr. Trevor just put in a call to that young lawyer Cynthia Thomas had mentored, and she took on every bureaucratic hoop and barrier with a gleeful tenacity that really endeared her to me.

No, the hardest part was demagicking the house.

Brianna had left behind the box that connected to the hidden library in Boston, and book by book, artifact by artifact, I sent her everything from our library and Miss Zenobia's office and the cellar. Even after all that was gone, I was still finding things in the parlor and the kitchen that I realized when I touched them had some sort of enchantment to them.

That was a thing I could do now. I could touch things and feel their stories. It wasn't the same as seeing the threads and examining the connecting nodes and larger webs, but the more I did it, the sharper the images became. I had no idea what possible use it would ever be, but since I wasn't fighting other witches anymore, it scarcely mattered.

As big a job as it was cleaning up the house, I managed to get it all sorted before the day Jackson Smith was scheduled to arrive. After all the interviews and home visits and background checks, I could scarcely believe it was finally happening.

By some quirk of fate, I had still never actually met the boy. Mr. Trevor had, and so had the lawyer, but not me.

Edward and Coco's great-grandson. I would never be able to explain to him our connection. Even if I could explain the magic, how could I burden him with the knowledge of just what I had given up just to be sure he was alive in this world? No kid should have to process that. And what a weird way to distort our relationship. No, all he would ever know was I was the young woman with some strange drive to take in misfit kids and help them become adults who could sort of fit in.

Yeah, I was going to have to work on the school motto. That was way too long to try to say it in Latin.

"Nervous?" Mr. Trevor asked. I thought he had been in his office, but apparently he had come down to watch me pace the foyer, stopping repeatedly to stare out the window next to the door.

"Maybe this was a mistake?" I said.

"Nonsense," he said. "This house was meant to be a school."

"But it wasn't a school," I said. "Not for the whole time you've been here."

"I know," he said. "But I always felt like it was longing for students to come back someday. And now they are."

I remembered the moment I had, oh so hesitantly, brought the idea up to him. I thought I was going to have to talk him into it, which was going to be tough since I wasn't sure myself it was a good idea.

I had nearly been knocked back by the shock wave of enthusiasm that erupted out of him. And by the looks of him now, none of that had diminished.

"Ah, here he comes now," Mr. Trevor said, and I spun to see Nick coming up the porch steps, a dark-haired little boy trailing along behind him. I swung the door open before he could even raise his hand to knock.

"Come in!" I said. Nick raised his eyebrows at my exuberant greeting, but turned to hold a guiding hand out to Jackson.

"Jackson, this is it," he said.

"This is a school?" Jackson said, craning his head to look up at the chandelier that hung over the foyer.

"Since eighteen-eighty... something," I said. "We can look it up later if you like."

"Look it up?" he said.

"In the library," I said. "There are some books in there on local history. Plus a lot of other dusty old things. But there're also a lot of empty shelves that you're going to help me fill."

"Me?" he said. He sounded equal parts excited and terrified.

"You," I said. "As my first student, I'm going to be relying on you to help me figure out how things should run here. I know some of the stuff we'll need, from my perspective, but I'm going to need a kid's perspective, too."

"Okay," he said. He still sounded wary.

"But no pressure," I said. "We're not going to start anything like classes until you're ready. First, summer is just beginning. And second, you've had a tough couple of months. Your job now is just to adjust to your new life here. I know when my life gets hard, I like to curl up in a window seat with endless cups of tea and a stack of books taller than you. What do you like to do?"

"I draw," he said with great hesitation.

"Actually, Nick already told me something like that. I didn't know if you liked pencils or ink or if you prefer to work digitally or what, so I might have gone overboard with the art supplies."

That put a gleam in his eyes, although he looked over to Nick to make sure that this was not a trick.

"I think you're going to like it here," Nick said. "And like I said, I'm just next door when you need to see a familiar face."

Jackson nodded and lifted one side of his mouth in something like a smile.

"Master Jackson," Mr. Trevor said, finally stepping forward. "I'm

Mr. Trevor. I'm what you'd call the steward of this old place. How would you like the grand tour?"

Jackson looked to Nick again, who gave him a nod. "Sure," he said.

"Boy, I hope I didn't miss anything magical," I said as the two of them disappeared up the stairs.

"I can't believe you're doing this," Nick said as we walked back to the kitchen.

"To be honest, I can't either," I said. "It was Brianna's idea, but it feels like something maybe Brianna should be doing, not me."

"You'll do fine," he said. "You said you weren't going to actually teach them, right?"

"Online school," I said. "It's all set up for this fall. Our lawyer found a few other kids who should be here before school starts. But I'm just here to supervise. And encourage. And smooth the path to whatever the kid in question ought to be in life."

"And you can tell what that is?" he asked, raising an eyebrow in a Sophie-like way.

"Well, I'm sure the kids know," I said. "Don't discourage me. Not now that it's too late to back out."

"I'm not," he said, raising his hands in mock surrender. "That was just my inelegant way of asking about…" He broke off, looking around all the kitchen doors before taking a step closer to me. "Your magic," he concluded.

"My magic," I said, looking him up and down. He clearly found that disconcerting, even more so when I moved even closer to him and put my hand on his chest. I could feel the outline of an object under his shirt. A charm meant for a bracelet, but he was wearing it around his neck like a protective amulet.

"What are you doing?" he asked.

"Shh," I said, closing my eyes and letting the picture form. "That's a four-leaf clover. From a charm bracelet."

"Good guess," he said.

"Your mother gave it to you before you went to Afghanistan. It was her mother's before that. Her mother had been wearing it the day she was on vacation in Florida and got caught in a riptide. It was a miracle that man saved her."

I didn't describe everything I was seeing. I could feel his grandmother's adolescent terror as she was pulled further and further from shore. As her muscles tired, and she knew she would slip under soon, and the water would close over her...

"Very good guess," Nick said, disrupting my vision.

"I'm making you uncomfortable," I said, stepping back.

"No, you weren't," he said, but I could see he had broken out into a cold sweat.

"It's just stories," I said. "I see the stories of things. And I have to tell you, most of them are pretty boring. Leave it to you to be wearing something so special."

"Yeah," he said, brushing his hand over the shirt that covered the charm. I was just turning towards the refrigerator when he said, so softly I almost missed it, "Brianna told me what you did."

"Brianna told you what now?" I asked, turning back.

"She told me that I was gone, like Jackson was gone, and that no one remembered me but you," he said. "You saved me the same way you saved Jackson."

"Not the same way," I said. "It wasn't like what you saw. I bargained for you."

"Your end of the bargain put you in danger," he said.

Just how much had Brianna told him?

"Yeah, well..." I said, but could find no more words.

I couldn't explain why he had been in danger in the first place without mentioning Edward, and I wasn't ready to talk to Nick about Edward. Not yet.

Nick felt the sudden awkwardness between us, even if he didn't know what had caused it. He looked around for some conversation-rerouting inspiration but found none. Finally, he managed, "I think Jackson is going to like it here."

"He certainly likes *you*," I said. "I hope you'll be stopping by a lot. At least until he and I manage to bond."

"Well, I was planning on doing that anyway," he said. "I *am* just next door."

"Yes, you are," I said.

The notification on my phone beeped, and I pulled it out of my pocket to glance at the screen. "Sophie and Brianna both. I better see what they want. Mr. Trevor's tour is going to end here with snacks. Can you take the tray out of the fridge for me? I have to run upstairs for a second."

"Sure," he said. "Trouble?"

"No," I said. "Just a social call. I think my days of trouble are behind me now."

He gave me a skeptical look, but I didn't stay to argue. I ran up the backstairs to the desk in my bedroom where my laptop was waiting.

And the moment I clicked into the virtual conference room, Brianna and Sophie were both waiting for me.

"This better not be imminent danger, because I just told Nick my trouble days were behind me and I'd hate for you two to make a liar out of me that quickly," I said, all in a rush. "But if it's imminent danger, my bugout bag is already packed. Where do I have to go? New Orleans? Boston?"

"Neither, girl," Sophie said. "We just wanted to say hi."

"Cause it's Jackson's first day!" Brianna said, hands in the air like she was at a rave.

"Yes, he's here," I said.

"Tell us all about it," Sophie said. "But start with Nick. How is Nick doing this lovely summer day?"

Yeah, there was no version of my life that didn't have Sophie teasing me about something. Even from twelve hundred miles away.

And Brianna was even further away. But the physical distance didn't matter. Even through cameras and computer monitors and videoconferencing software, I could feel them reaching out to me through our magical bond, and I reached back.

Nothing was ever going to break up the Witches Three.

THE VIKING WITCH COZY
MYSTERIES

In case you missed it, check out Body at the Crossroads, the first book
in the Viking Witch Cozy Mystery Series!

When her mother dies after a long illness, Ingrid Torfa must sell the
family home to cover the medical bills. Her career as a book illus-
trator not yet exactly launched, Ingrid faces two options: live in her
battered old Volkswagen, or go back to her mother's small town in
northern Minnesota.

The small town that still haunts her dreams more than a decade
since she last visited it. Or rather, not the town but the grandmother.

All of the drawings she fills notebooks with witches and the trolls
that do their bidding? Not as whimsical in her nightmares as she
sketches them in the bright light of day.

If not for her beloved cat Mjolner, living in the Volkswagen just
might tempt her.

But the cat wants four walls and a door, so north she goes. And
finds trouble in the form of a dead body before she even finds her
grandmother's little town. How much can a town of stoic fishermen
possibly be hiding?

As Ingrid is about to find out, quite a lot.

Body at the Crossroads, the first book in the Viking Witch Cozy Mystery Series!

THE WEAL & WOE BOOKSHOP
WITCH MYSTERIES

In case you missed it, check out The Teashop Terror, the first book in the new Weal & Woe Bookshop Witch Mystery Series!

No one knows more about every branch of magic than Tabitha Greene. She devoted years to studying the most esoteric texts, hunting down the most obscure source materials, and deciphering the most cryptic ancient scrolls. But her career in academia hits a dead end when no wizard will take her on as an apprentice.

Just because, despite being descended from two long and prestigious lines of witches, her attempts to actually perform any magic always fail. Often spectacularly.

But no more college means no more dorm life. And no magical skills means no real job skills, at least, not in the witchy world. And a life spent moving from school to school every few months was a life without real friendships. She finds herself alone with nowhere to go.

Then an uncle she barely remembers offers her a summer job, running his bookstore over the summer. The Weal and Woe Bookstore, located in a magical pocket world within a block of buildings just north of the old Mill District of Minneapolis, Minnesota.

Not exactly the pinnacle of all her hopes and dreams. But it's just for one summer, right?

Or so Tabitha tells herself. But unbeknownst to her, the Weal and Woe Bookstore is about to change her life.

The Teashop Terror, the first book in the new Weal & Woe Bookshop Witch Mystery Series!

ALSO FROM RATATOSKR PRESS

The Ritchie and Fitz Sci-Fi Murder Mysteries starts with Murder on the Intergalactic Railway.

For Murdina Ritchie, acceptance at the Oymyakon Foreign Service Academy means one last chance at her dream of becoming a diplomat for the Union of Free Worlds. For Shackleton Fitz IV, it represents his last chance not to fail out of military service entirely.

Strange that fate should throw them together now, among the last group of students admitted after the start of the semester. They had once shared the strongest of friendships. But that all ended a long time ago.

But when an insufferable but politically important woman turns up murdered, the two agree to put their differences aside and work together to solve the case.

Because the murderer might strike again. But more importantly, solving a murder would just have to impress the dour colonel who clearly thinks neither of them belong at his academy.

Murder on the Intergalactic Railway, the first book in the Ritchie and Fitz Sci-Fi Murder Mysteries, available everywhere books are sold.

FREE EBOOK!

Like exclusive, free content?

If you'd like to receive "A Collection of Witchy Prequels", a free collection of short story prequels to the Witches Three Cozy Mystery and Viking Witch Cozy Mystery series, as well as other free stories throughout the year, go to my website CateMartin.com to subscribe to my newsletter! This eBook is exclusively for newsletter subscribers and will never be sold in stores. Check it out!

ABOUT THE AUTHOR

Cate Martin has written stories which have appeared in *Mystery, Crime and Mayhem* quarterly magazine as well as in the annual *Holiday Spectacular* Advent calendar of Christmas stories. She is also the author of three witch mystery series: *The Witches Three Cozy Mysteries*, and *The Viking Witch Cozy Mysteries* and *The Weal and Woe Bookshop Witch Mysteries*. She currently lives in Minneapolis, Minnesota. You can learn more about her work at CateMartin.com.

ALSO BY CATE MARTIN

The Witches Three Cozy Mystery Series

Charm School

Work Like a Charm

Third Time is a Charm

Old World Charm

Charm his Pants Off

Charm Offensive

The Witches Three Cozy Mysteries Books 1-3

The Witches Three Cozy Mysteries Books 4-6

The Viking Witch Cozy Mystery Series

Body at the Crossroads

Death Under the Bridge

Murder on the Lake

Killing in the Village Commons

Bloodshed in the Forest

Corpse in the Mead Hall

Slaying on the Lake Shore

Bones by the Forest Road

Sacrifice Behind the Falls

Body Under the Café

Assassination in the Glade

Bewitchment After the Storm (available July 9, 2024 direct from me or August 13, 2024 in stores everywhere)

The Viking Witch Cozy Mysteries Books 1-3

The Viking Witch Cozy Mysteries Books 4-6

The Weal & Woe Bookshop Witch Mystery Series

The Teashop Terror

The Salon & Spa Scandal

The Bookseller Blunder

The Entrepreneur Enigma

The Novelty Shop Nightmare (available August 13, 2024 direct from me or September 10, 2024 in stores everywhere)

The Courtyard Conundrum (available December 10, 2024 direct from me or January 14, 2025 in stores everywhere)